What People Are Saying About

The Sheep Thief

"Truly Tremendous, I loved it. Power, Love and Wisdom flood the reader's mind in this tremendous story by Al Walker."

—Charles "Tremendous" Jones, author

"When you are ready to make the move from mediocrity to a life of fulfillment and success, then you must read, apply and live *The Sheep Thief* today—and if you aren't ready, this wonderful book by my friend Al Walker will get you ready."

—Zig Ziglar, author

"If you know there is something more to this life and you just don't know how to find it, *The Sheep Thief* is your guide to discovering the life you were meant to live."

—Stephen Arterburn, author

"This book will nurture your soul, nourish your mind and warm your heart. Read it for inspiration. Study it for education. Refer to it often for maximum application."

—Nido Qubein, author
President, High Point University
Chairman, Great Harvest Bread Co.

"Highly recommend reading for everyone! This book encourages and teaches proven steps to success—mentally, physically and spiritually. Written with heart, depth, humor and real life experiences!"

—Joanne Wallace, conference speaker & author

"The words in this fabulous book, *The Sheep Thief*, are a compilation of ideas most needed in our world today. It is a must-read!"

—Bob and Jane Handly, authors
Beyond Fear and
Getting Unstuck

"*The Sheep Thief* by Al Walker is a wonderfully uplifting message of hope, challenge and achievement that is timeless. Most of us can identify with the frustrations faced by Harvey and Jean and can travel with them on their journey. More than a feel-good experience, however, this book provides solid, proven principles and techniques that will help you move up the stairway to an exemplary life that provides satisfaction and success in more ways than you can imagine."

—George Morrisey, speaker/consultant
Author, *Morrisey on Planning* three-book series

"*The Sheep Thief* is a hidden opportunity for anyone needing a turning point in his or her life. Al has brought the Master's hand into this story."

—Tom Winninger, author

"You, too, can overcome bland ambitions as you experience the powerful ideas in this timely book by Al Walker. The story will draw you in. The message will draw you out to make new choices and confront your own possibilities!"

—Elizabeth Jeffries, CSP, CPAE
Author, *The Heart of Leadership: How to Inspire, Encourage and Motivate People to Follow You*

"This powerful story provides inspiration and direction while being an intriguing story to read. Sort of like having a mentor coach on your bookshelf. Don't miss it."

—Floyd Wickman, CSP, CPAE
Author, *Letters to Linda* and coauthor of *Mentoring*

"*The Sheep Thief* is a book that will inspire you, encourage you and enlighten you! Al Walker has written a powerful book that will bless you and help you to achieve greater results in your personal and professional lives. I highly recommend you read this book, then reread it and you will be blessed!"

—Willie Jolley
Author, *It Only Takes a Minute to Change Your Life* and *A Setback Is a Setup for a Comeback!*

"Al Walker has created an unusually reliable format combining allegory, analogy and anecdote coupled with research and personal history—all of this makes this book exciting reading, potentially long remembered and life impacting."

—Dave Yoho, author

"Remarkable! Transformational! This book will lead you into a life-changing perspective on your purpose and your calling for the 21st century."

—Glenna Salsbury
CSP, CPAE Speaker Hall of Fame
Author, *The Art of the Fresh Start*

"Al Walker has combined his years of experience and wisdom to create a masterful new book. When you apply the principles contained in Mr. Taylor's Tool Kit, you, too, will overcome your bland ambitions."

—Stephen C. Tweed, CSP
Chairman & CEO
Lighthouse Learning Systems

The Sheep Thief

The Sheep Thief

How Anyone, Anywhere, Can Make a Positive Change in Life

AL WALKER, CSP, CPAE

THE SHEEP THIEF

Published by
Tremendous Life Books
118 West Allen Street
Mechanicsburg, PA 17055

ISBN: 978-1-933715-91-9

Printed in the United States of America

QUOTABLE QUOTES

"In the long run, men hit only what they aim at. Therefore, they had better aim at something high."

—Henry David Thoreau

"Aim at the heavens and set standards and goals that in the beginning will seem beyond reach. Enjoy the challenges this brings and don't look for perfection. One day you might get close to it. If on the other hand, you aim low, that is where you will always be."

—Frank Fools Crow
1890–1989
Ceremonial Chief of the Teton Sioux
Healer & Holy Man

"We must build—with every thought, word and action, or we must destroy with every thought, word or action. Since we cannot live in neutral, there is no in-between."

—Joe Batten, CPAE
1926–2006
Author of 19 books on leadership
Member, Speakers Hall of Fame

"It's not that we want too much. It's that we settle for too little."

—Anonymous

"...but for a line, be that sublime. Not failure, but low aim is crime."

—Socrates

CONTENTS

Foreword 13

Acknowledgments and Appreciation 15

Dedication 16

The Parable of the Sheep Thief 17

PART I—THE ENCOUNTER

I. The Final Straw 23

II. Confronting the Enemy: Sometimes Yourself 29

III. Meeting Seth Taylor 35

IV. Stairway to the Stars 42

V. Laying the Foundation: The Attitude Factor 50

VI. The First Steps: Faith—Believe the Dream 55

VII. The Steps Get Steeper 95

VIII. Finishing the Climb 114

IX. Beyond the Door 133

X. Summary of Steps 140

PART II—MR. TAYLOR'S LEADERSHIP TOOL KIT

XI. The Meeting 145

XII. 45 Team-Building Ideas 148

XIII. Seven Timeless Truths for the Leader of the Future 159

XIV. Harvey Cole Today 161

About Joe Batten 163

About Al Walker 164

FOREWORD

"On the Plains of Hesitation bleach the bones of countless millions, who, at the Dawn of Victory, sat down to wait, and waiting they died."

—George W. Cecil

The people who consistently win in their life endeavors are not a part of the "let's wait" mob. Winners attack... They charge... They do. They understand that the joys encountered along the road leading from cradle to grave are the result of LIVING, not merely existing.

The "let's wait" folks were born into mediocrity and then had a relapse. They're walking around looking for a place to plug in and hold on. They're the people who go looking for a job, spot the name of some big corporation sitting on top of a tall building and think to themselves, "Aha!!! The mother ship!" It's here they plug in and hold on—simply surviving.

The author of this inspiring book, Al Walker, and the man who encouraged Al to "Walkerize" it, are winners who never waited for things to happen. They're warriors who attack life, love abundantly and have given truckloads of themselves, their time, their energy and their wisdom. As a result, they've accomplished much.

As you challenge yourself to explore the pages that follow, you'll need a couple of really big buckets to catch all the goodies in store for you. And please note, I said, **CHALLENGE YOURSELF**. Take the time to complete the steps as an exercise in unlocking all your possibilities. Of course, you can just read and enjoy and learn. Please don't rob yourself by just reading. Give yourself the gift Al wants so much for you to have. Please... "Do" the book, for the great aim of education is not knowledge but action. Over the years, I've cheated myself out of bigger wins, bigger celebrations and a bigger net worth by reading the best advice from top performers and then doing nothing with it. It's simply easier to store words of great wisdom into the "nice to know" category than it is to do...to take action.

Doing! Acting! Having! Being! That's what this book is all about. It's about giving with no strings attached and, as a result, putting the Law of Multiplied Return to work for a more prosperous harvest. The Law is working for you right now. It's delivering to you exactly what you've ordered. If you're not really happy with what you have or with what seems to continue to come your way, take an honest and hard look at what you're giving out. It is a fact of life, like it or not, that what we give out...what we plant, we **ALWAYS GET BACK AND IN A MULTIPLIED MANNER**.

Al has put together for you a huge truckload of gems...truths that when acted upon, when planted and nurtured in the very core of your being, will deliver a wonderfully prosperous harvest. Read the book. "Do" the book and enjoy the harvest...the harvest of a happier and more abundant life.

On the platform built for winners
Stand the champions who chose to "do."
They opened the door to opportunity,
Met the challenge, sprouted wings and flew.

Bob Johnson
Sydney, Australia

ACKNOWLEDGMENTS AND APPRECIATION

With deepest appreciation and thanks to Margaret Muir (1950–2003) for her editing skills and her willingness to retype this manuscript umpteen zillion times—OK, maybe a dozen or so—but it seemed like umpteen zillion. Regretfully, "Moo," as she was affectionately known, was an integral part of Al Walker and Associates for over eighteen years and didn't live to see this book published.

To all the folks who pored over the manuscript and gave me advice—all of which was used. They include Al's wife Margaret, who is the world's greatest English teacher; Jim Hicks, an old friend; Charlie Farrell and Pete Stursberg (1938–1999); Libby Bernardine, a teacher at the University of South Carolina and a wonderful editor; Rev. Marshall Edwards, Al's former pastor; Bob Johnson, who wrote the foreword and is the individual who first shared the Sheep Thief story with Al way back in 1974, plus the friends who shared their ideas and their wisdom so it could be passed on to you.

DEDICATION
Earby Albert Walker Jr.

To my father, Earby Albert Walker, Jr. (1924–1974), who was a saint and a survivor. But more important, he loved the Lord and led us in the way we should go. He never quit, and he never bailed out. He was an encourager who always expected the best—out of himself and everyone else. He loved to laugh, to tell or hear a good joke or story and to sing, which he did often. He passed all of those characteristics on to his children, one of whom is the author of this book and his oldest son, who to this day loves him dearly and is proud to be his namesake.

And to
JOE BATTEN

Without whom this book probably would never have been written. Joe Batten called Al Walker and asked if he'd be interested in a story line that he wanted to pass on to Al to be (as Joe put it) "Walkerized." Al agreed, and they went to work. Joe created the initial story line about two people working together. Al added the parable of the sheep thief, the character of Mr.Taylor and the rest of the book.

This book has been several years in the writing, rewriting and more rewriting. Its strong spiritual base is a result of Al's values, lifestyle and level of commitment to his Creator and Savior, Jesus Christ. May this book be a blessing to all who read it. May it reinforce those who are strong in their walk, and may it give a sense of direction to any who might have lost their way.

THE PARABLE OF THE SHEEP THIEF

Several hundred years ago in a quaint village in Italy, two young men were caught stealing sheep. They were immediately taken to trial before the town judge, found guilty and, there in front of their fellow villagers, were given their sentence. It was a cruel, harsh and painful sentence that would mark them for life. It was ordered that both young men be branded on the forehead with the letters **ST**—for sheep thief. Those who sat in judgment wanted to make sure that, for the rest of their lives, these young men, their fellow villagers and anyone who looked the two thieves in the face would be reminded of their crime and know that anyone who committed such a crime would be branded for life.

Not long after the punishment had been administered, one of the young men immediately left town telling everyone he was going to get as far away from them as his legs would carry him. However, in every village he went, word would spread within a few days that a sheep thief was among them and he'd move on to the next village. He spent the rest of his life moving from place to place. Finally, years later, he died a lonely, embarrassed and embittered old man who was far away from home, penniless and without any friends.

The other young man wanted to run away also but decided to stay, face the music, make amends and straighten his life out. He decided to give himself completely to his family, his friends and his village. He even worked as a shepherd for the man from whom he had stolen the sheep and eventually earned enough money to pay him back for the sheep he'd stolen. Then he saved enough to buy a small tract of land. He acquired a few sheep and started his own flock.

Each year he would add more sheep. He carefully tended to them as he added more and more sheep over the years, and within a couple of decades, he owned the largest flocks of sheep in the area. Looking out across the hills around the village, his flocks looked like huge patches of snow as you gazed from hill to hill. They numbered in the thousands, and he employed over 75 sheepherders alone. He was very active in his church and in his community, giving generously to others in need.

When he first started out he would sell his wool to various weavers, but eventually he started his own weaving plant in the village, using the wool from his vast herds. His business ventures created an empire that eventually employed several hundred people. The village grew, and the fine woolen cloth it produced became popular all over the world. The man who once was a sheep thief had become the wealthiest, most successful man in the region. Everyone knew his name and honored him. He became the patriarch. There was not one human being who had not been touched by him in some way.

Many years later, as this now compassionate, caring and powerful man was walking down the sidewalk, a visitor to the village passed him. All this visitor saw was a weathered but distinguished-looking old man with a scar on his forehead that looked somewhat like the letters **ST**. As he walked by the old man, he saw a bent-over, elderly shopkeeper sweeping in front of his store and the visitor asked him, "I noticed the letters **ST** on the forehead of the gentleman who just passed by. Why does he have that on his forehead, and what do those letters stand for?"

The shopkeeper watched as the old sheep thief stopped at stores along his way and shook hands with those he met. He thought back on the crime the sheep thief had committed so long ago when they were both so young. But before the words "sheep thief" came out of his mouth, he thought about the wonderful life his friend had lived, all the people he'd helped, the success he had enjoyed and the leadership he'd brought to the village. What the shopkeeper said next was a testimony to a changed life.

The shopkeeper looked at the visitor and with a broad smile said, "You mean him? The one with the **ST** on his forehead?"

"Yes," said the visitor. The shopkeeper paused and then, slowly, smiling and nodding his head, said, "The **ST**? ... It stands for **SAINT**."

PART I
THE ENCOUNTER

CHAPTER I
THE FINAL STRAW

At exactly 9:00 a.m. Friday morning, the staff meeting adjourned. The seven people sitting around the table pushed their chairs back, picked up their notes, their organizers, their laptop computers, their coffee mugs and whatever other paraphernalia they had brought with them to at least give them the appearance of being on top of things and headed out the door of Conference Room 7-B, which overlooked the city's skyline from the 20th floor of the Battle Building at the corner of Blanding Avenue and King Street. Harvey Cole had hardly said a word during the entire meeting. He'd gone in the door a little over an hour ago on cloud 9... He even felt like he was floating as he'd entered the room. When this meeting started he was higher than a kite. Now he was leaving the meeting feeling lower than low, and he was literally seething inside. On top of all that, nobody would even make eye contact with Harvey as they left the room. He felt abandoned, alone and embarrassed.

When he finally got to his office, he calmly closed his door, walked behind his desk, then in an explosion of anger, jerked his chair out and sat down hard as he slammed his armload of "stuff" back on top of all the other mess on his desk. For the first time since he had heard the announcement, he let his emotions show. Harvey gritted his teeth and let out a low, angry, guttural kind of growl that slowly seeped out of his mouth. Now he was mad on top of being about as down in the dumps as he'd ever felt, and he knew why...as all of the negative events in his life replayed themselves in his mind: disappointment over losing a major service contract earlier in the week, having a couple of run-ins with Dianne, one of his team members he'd never gotten along with and things had gotten a little caustic. The problems he was having with his oldest son Kevin had stolen every last drop of his energy and his drive…until this morning when he came to work expecting to finally have something very positive happen in his life.

For the past year since Harvey's wife had decided to leave him, his kids had been acting up. He had two sons and a baby daughter who now lived with his ex-wife and her new husband. He saw them every other weekend and almost every Wednesday night when he was in town. Lately, his sixteen-year-old son Kevin, the oldest, had been hanging out with the wrong crowd and seemed to be withdrawing more and more into himself.

Harvey felt totally overwhelmed. Not just today. For the past several days and even weeks, he felt like all the drive had gone out of his life. Everything seemed cloudy and dull. He felt listless and just had absolutely no energy at all. He didn't know what to do next, yet he knew he had to "mush on." He had too many responsibilities not to.

His emotions were a mixture of anger on one hand and self-pity on the other. He felt like throwing in the towel. Only in his mid-forties, Harvey had just found out he'd been passed over for a promotion he thought he had in the bag. Even with all his troubles, he'd gone into that meeting this morning with high expectations. He knew the job was his. Yesterday, when he'd heard that Doc Henry, the company president himself, was going to attend, he knew the only reason Doc would be showing up would be because he wanted to personally announce that his longtime friend whom he had brought into the business over fifteen years ago, Mr. Harvey Cole, would now be the new director of operations.

Harvey had been thinking about his new title and all the perks it would bring ever since Bryan Petty's unexpected resignation a couple of weeks ago. The raise and the elevation in prestige would solve most of his other problems. Then—BOOM—like a thief in the night, the rug had been jerked out from under his feet. He'd been right about one thing. Doc Henry was there to make the announcement all right…just not the one he'd planned on hearing.

When the meeting started, Doc went on and on about what a wonderful individual the next director of operations was. How that individual had risen to be one of the top project managers the company had ever had. He talked about what a positive impact this new director would have on operations and what a feather in the company's cap it was to have a person of this caliber, this level of integrity, this wisdom and this proven success at the helm of operations. He talked about how the company's clients would have even more confidence in their projects coming in on time and under budget now that this new director was in place. Harvey was smiling.

When Doc finished gushing, Harvey's jaw dropped and everyone noticed. Did he hear his name come out of his old buddy's mouth? Nope, he heard her name, Mrs. Jean Bennett, a thirty-five-year-old human rocket, who was at least ten years his junior and who seemed to be zooming her way to the top. Now Harvey was experiencing even more feelings of rejection and futility than he ever imagined he could endure ever since the announcement had been made a little less than an hour ago. Everybody had been all smiles as they congratulated Jean on her latest step up the corporate ladder. Harvey had regained his composure and even smiled and nodded at Jean when he left the room, even though his insides were in knots. He honestly felt like he had taken a hard punch in his stomach. This latest news really was the final straw.

All day long he wallowed in self-pity. "Am I burned out?" Harvey wondered. "Am I over the hill? Am I just not good enough? Am I not smart enough? Why do I keep on trying? What's the use?" His anger raised its head for the umpteenth time that day. He slammed his fist down on his desk and thought, "How could they do that to me? Who in the world did they think they were? Not to even give me a chance. I deserved a shot at that job." Harvey knew he'd pushed his blood pressure to the limit, and he kept it there most of the day.

Even through lunch he thought about his failures and what a disaster his life had been. He ate lunch in his office, all by himself with the door closed. The last thing he wanted to hear was any comments about how wonderful Jean Bennett was, what a great choice they'd made, how much people in their department were looking forward to working with her…and on and on and on. He also didn't want to hear any words of consolation from the two or three co-workers who knew he thought he had the promotion in the bag.

He tried hard to generate some anger at Jean, but strangely enough, he couldn't work up any real resentment toward her personally. Harvey knew the decision had been made way up the chain of command, not just by Doc, but also by the members of the board of directors. It wasn't Jean's fault. Jean Bennett really was someone you just couldn't help but like. Upbeat, positive and energetic, she seemed a born winner. Harvey was angry all right, but not at Jean. Oh, maybe a little…but it was more jealousy and envy toward Jean than anything else. He was angry at the company, at the president of the company and those heartless management gorillas who had passed him over. He was angry at the world, at his place in the world and at himself. But for some reason, he wasn't angry at Jean. He knew Jean was a hard worker. What made the whole thing even more interesting was that he and Jean were also friends—good friends—and they had worked together for over seven years. Even though they hadn't done a lot of work together lately, Harvey was still confident of their friendship. He also knew he'd seen a change in Jean over the past two to three years. She was different now, more confident, more in control. Jean had always had a strong personal presence, but now she had an even stronger sense of purpose. Not only was she attractive but she had an inner beauty that came through loud and clear when you were around her. "Today's promotion would give her even more to be proud of or to gloat over," Harvey thought to himself for just a second—even though he knew Jean wasn't like that at all.

At four o'clock that Friday afternoon after stewing all day, Harvey finally made a decision. He needed to talk to Jean. He needed to congratulate her, but he also wanted just to visit with an old friend who had earned her day in the sun. Logic told him there had to be a reason Jean had been promoted over him even though he could not see it. Now that Jean had the promotion, Harvey knew he should talk to her. Jean and her husband Chuck were close, and their families had been close before Harvey's divorce and still were to some extent. If it weren't for all that, he'd just pat Jean on the back, congratulate her and try to move on.

But this relationship was different. It was business **AND** it was personal. They'd all spent many hours discussing every aspect of their lives. Their families had vacationed together, spent many an hour in each other's homes and also attended the same church. Chuck and Harvey had even been classmates in college. They knew more about each other than some members of their own families knew. Jean was a friend, and he knew he could count on her. She'd heard him talk about wanting that promotion, so she knew how he felt. He also knew she was the kind of person who would give him plenty of space, but if she'd not heard from him in a day or two, she'd make contact and share a conciliatory thought or two with him...not in a patronizing or condescending kind of way, but out of love and appreciation for their friendship.

The more Harvey thought about Jean, the more he realized she seemed to have some things going for her that he didn't have. He wanted to know what her "secret" was. What was it that Jean had that he didn't have? What had Jean done that he hadn't done? What had Jean done to get her where she was today?

Harvey knew the truth. Even though it was hard to accept, he knew he had to either be satisfied with his station in life or he had to make some changes. If he wanted to get out of the rut he was apparently in, he had to do something different. He chuckled when he remembered that the definition of insanity was when you keep doing the same things over and over expecting different results. He thought of a comment one of his old high school coaches had made to him one time about "luck." He had told Harvey that luck was when preparation met opportunity. Harvey knew he was at a major crossroad in his life. He had to just accept things the way they were, do his time, get his check and go into a survival mode OR he had to prepare himself to be ready for the *next* opportunity if another one came along.

He began to feel a little better about himself and couldn't decide if it was because the weekend was here and he knew he'd be getting out of this place for a few days or if it was because he felt himself leaning in the direction of doing something about his somewhat bland lot in life. He felt this compelling need to talk to someone who could help him, who knew him, who had been in the trenches with him, who'd been there in both good and bad times and who would listen to him with an open mind. Strangely enough, the person whose name would not leave his mind and whom he'd been through a lot with was just the person he needed to talk to—his longtime friend and the new director of operations, Jean Bennett.

CHAPTER II
CONFRONTING THE ENEMY: SOMETIMES YOURSELF

He immediately picked up the phone, buzzed Jean's number and, as soon as Jean picked up the phone—even before she could say "Hello"—Harvey said, "Hello, Jean." Jean responded in her usual friendly way, "Hi, Harvey. I wondered who that was," she said with a smile in her voice. "How are you doing?"

"I'm doing great," Harvey lied. Then he said, "Congratulations again on your promotion. I know it's something you've really wanted. I really am proud of you, Jean. This is not only great for you, though. I know it's a good move for the company and for your family."

"Thanks, Harvey. I feel bad because I know you wanted a shot at this job, and I don't know if I really wanted it or not—I even thought you'd be the one to get it. But if they think that's where I can do the best job, I'm willing to give it 110 percent."

Harvey's cynicism kicked in briefly as he thought, "Sure, Ms. Altruistic, just keep on being so accommodating. That's an easy attitude when everything always goes the way you want it to." But instead, what came out of his mouth was, "Well, I know you'll do a terrific job." Now Harvey felt ashamed for feeling the way he'd felt toward someone who had often gone out of her way to be a friend to him. Harvey went on to say, "Jean, I'd like to visit with you maybe sometime next week when it's convenient for you. I really need to talk to you."

"Sure," she said, "Why wait? How about right now?"

Harvey hadn't planned on that, so he stumbled through a weak "OK."

Jean said, "I'm on the way," and she hung up the phone.

As Harvey put his phone back down, he shook his head and thought, "Dadgummit, I don't really want to talk with her right now. I wanted to get out of here." He felt his anger resurfacing, but then he quickly thought, "How can you get mad at someone who always seems so willing to help at a moment's notice, who not only wants to help but also makes you feel like you just made her day worthwhile by even asking her for some help?" Jean was in Harvey's office and settled down in a chair with her legs crossed and her hands in her lap in less than five minutes.

Jean reiterated how she'd been caught off guard when Doc Henry had first approached her a couple of weeks earlier to discuss this opportunity with her. She said what surprised her was that she really had thought Harvey would be the one getting the promotion. She apologized for not saying anything earlier, but Doc had sworn her to secrecy until he could make the announcement himself. She told Harvey how their friendship was more important to her than any job she could ever have. Harvey agreed and again lied and told her he was OK. After they had chatted some more about Jean's new job and she had asked for Harvey's opinion on several new challenges she knew she'd be facing, Jean stopped talking almost in mid-sentence, looked squarely at Harvey, took a deep breath, smiled and said, "I'm sorry, Harvey. Here I am going on and on about some of the things that are on my mind, and you're the one who wanted to talk. What's on your mind?"

Even though he was controlled in his speech, an observer could have seen and heard the emotion as Harvey blurted out all of his pent-up frustrations by saying, "To use an old cliché, I suppose I'm just burned out. Nothing seems to be working out for me. Everybody else seems to be moving onward and upward but me. I'm almost at the point where I want to fill up my car with gas, get out on the highway, see how far it will take me and start over wherever I stop. Once again, I've been passed over for a promotion. I feel like I'm a branded man in this outfit. I'd probably be better off if I quit and moved on to something else."

Jean didn't say a word. After a couple of seconds she sat up on the edge of her chair, brushed her hand back through her hair, hesitated for another moment and then—looking off as almost in a daze, and very seriously but almost in a whisper—said softly, "Harvey, three years ago I was just as frustrated and discouraged as you appear to be right now. I was fortunate enough to meet a man who literally changed my life."

"Does Chuck know about this other man?"

Jean smiled, "Yes, and he approves of him wholeheartedly. Let me tell you what happened.

"As you know, you and I have several things in common. I know you remember us discussing how in my mid-twenties, a few years before I met Chuck and before I came to work here, I went through a very difficult divorce that I didn't want. It cost me a lot of money, and I knew my whole future with my two children would change because I couldn't be with them every day. My first husband, who had been my high school sweetheart, had decided to leave me for another woman. During the divorce hearings he succeeded in getting joint custody, which meant now I would have to share my precious children with some woman I didn't know. Also, I hated my job and the people I was working with so I quit.

"It didn't take me long to realize I couldn't make it on what little savings I had. Even with the child support payments I was getting, I knew I had to go back to work. Luckily, because of my engineering background, I was able to get a job here fairly quickly. It seemed like I was permanently in survival mode the first few years I was here. Remember how unhappy I was a few years back when we were working together on the Water View project and how they'd pulled me off that job just as it was beginning to take shape and put me on that smaller Briargate job? The only explanation I ever got was that they didn't feel they needed me there anymore. What galled me was I had been the one who'd birthed that baby we called Water View to begin with. I remember thinking about all the work I'd put into the project and how I wouldn't be around to see it finished. When that happened on top of all my other troubles, I felt like running away myself. I wanted to do EXACTLY what you just described—tell them to stick it in their ear, take off down the interstate and start over wherever I ran out of gas. The only thing that held me back was the love I have for my two children, Amy and Janna. That's when I stumbled across Mr. Taylor. Or, I should say, Mr. Taylor stumbled across me.

"I was sitting in my office late one afternoon staring out the window thinking about the shambles my personal and business life were in and contemplating my trip to 'wherever I ran out of gas' if I could just figure out a way to steal my own children, when I was disturbed by someone knocking on my door saying, 'Mind if I come in?' And there, standing in my doorway, was an older man, probably in his mid-sixties with white hair, a thick white mustache, wire-frame bifocals and a smile that would melt an iceberg. He was wearing a dark blue suit with a vest, a crisp white shirt with monogrammed cuff links, and he was looking at a pocket watch he held in his hand while the other end of the chain was attached to a watch fob through a buttonhole on his vest.

"As I sat there in my misery thinking how I really didn't want to be bothered by anybody, much less some old codger like this, I said, 'Sure. Come on in.' He put the watch back in his vest pocket, stuck out his hand, which I instinctively grabbed as we shook hands, and said 'Hello, Jean. I'm on the board of directors here at Millspring.' As he talked, he brought up some of the projects I had worked on, the positive impact I'd had on the company and the good relationship I had with my other team members. I remember thinking how impressed I was with how much he knew about me—he'd done his homework.

"He told me he'd heard I'd been down in the dumps lately and that I might need somebody to talk to. I thought, 'Who is this guy?' I'd never met him before, and now he stumbles into my office and wants me to pour my heart out. Give me a break! I'd never even seen him before, and now he wants to just waltz right in here and cheer me up. My first reaction was to toss him out on his ear. 'I'll be nice though since he is on the board, but just nice enough to get him out of here.' But then for some unexplainable reason we began talking, and within just a short period of time I felt I'd known him for years.

"He was so easy to talk to. I felt comfortable—really comfortable. The chemistry between us was magical. It wasn't anything physical…at least not 'that' kind of physical, just comfortable…like I remembered feeling as a child when I would talk with my dad. I talked; he listened. But he did more than listen. He encouraged with his eyes, his facial expression. He had a strong personal presence the likes of which I'd never seen before. He exuded quiet confidence. Have you ever met anybody like that, Harvey?"

Harvey chuckled and said, "No, I obviously don't know for sure, but this guy sounds like a dressed-up grandpa or maybe even Santa Claus to me." They both laughed and then Jean said, "Before I tell you any more about him, tell me how you're feeling right now—right at this moment. I need for you to be as specific as you can, Harvey."

As they talked, Harvey reminded Jean of his overall situation and how he really was so disappointed, frustrated and somewhat embarrassed. He reiterated his desire to take off for parts unknown.

He told Jean how he felt like a failure and that he hated

to admit his job wasn't going well. They both knew Harvey had failed at making his marriage work. Jean and her husband had been there throughout that entire messy ordeal. On top of everything else, Harvey was having a tough time financially. The more he talked, the more convinced he was that going to another city, another job and another group of people would solve his problems, even if it meant not seeing his children as much as he would like. When he finally finished pouring his heart out, Jean smiled one of her genuine, I-really-do-care-about-you-I've-been-there-and-I-want-to-help-ease-your-pain smiles of hers, and then she quietly shared the parable of the sheep thief with Harvey that Mr. Taylor shared with her the first time they met.

CHAPTER III
MEETING SETH TAYLOR

After Jean finished telling Harvey the parable, they both just sat there in total silence. After what seemed like an eternity, Harvey put his hand on his forehead and, with closed eyes, rubbed it as if he had a headache. But Jean knew it was the look of someone deep in thought. A minute or two later as Harvey opened his eyes, Jean said, "After Mr. Taylor shared that story with me, we began to meet regularly and, in fact, met several more times over the next few weeks. During our times together, he guided, challenged and helped me to completely overhaul and renew my whole life, including my mind, my body and my wounded spirit, and be more like the sheep thief who'd stayed home and turned his life around. I knew after being with Mr. Taylor I'd never be the same again. I really became a new person. He challenged me to overhaul and renew every dimension of my life...and, I mean EVERY dimension. It was a lot of work, but it was worth it. Harvey, you're only forty-five, and this guy told me of others he's helped who ranged in age from their teens to their umpteens. Maybe if you talked to him, he could give you some more objective insight. Would you like to meet him?"

"I'm not sure. I know I need to do something different, Jean, and I know no one ever gets too old to change, but maybe I'm too old to change enough for it to have a significant impact on my life. Maybe I don't have the energy or the inclination to—as they say—shoot for the stars," Harvey said uncertainly, looking at the floor. You could hear the self-pity in his voice. Jean knew that wasn't like him. She knew Harvey had always been steady as a rock—consistent, loyal and definitely a team player; he had just never shown a lot of drive and ambition.

Jean suddenly grinned and went on, "According to Mr. Taylor, chronological age really has nothing to do with our ability to change our lives. You can change if you DECIDE to, but simply WANTING to change won't do it. I don't know how many times he told me, 'Wanting isn't enough. You've got to take action,' and then he'd say with emphasis, 'AND you must take action TODAY,'" she said as her voice got louder and louder.

"Listen, Jean, *Dead Poets Society* was one of my all-time favorite movies." Harvey mumbled and went on in a staccato kind of way, "Carpe diem, carpe diem, carpe diem…I know… Seize the day."

Harvey thought for a moment, then sat up straighter in his chair. With a hint of determination in his voice, he stood on his self-pity and said, "OK. I obviously haven't been able to come up with what I ought to do, so lead me to him! If anybody needs…how did you say it, 'overhauling and renewing'…it's me. When can I see him?"

"I don't know," Jean said. "Let's call him."

"Call him?" Harvey repeated. "You mean just pick up the phone and tell a member of the board of directors I want to meet with him?"

"Yes, he works up on the 25th floor," Jean said, nodding her head. "You know—the executive floor. I never met with him there, but his extension is 2577. All I ever had to do was just buzz him, and he was always willing to set a time to meet me."

"Hold on, not so fast," Harvey said. "It's already 5:15 and I'm late getting out of here now. I have a few things to wrap up before I can leave, though. I'll call him first thing Monday morning. What was that extension again?"

"OK, but promise me you'll call?"

Harvey raised his eyebrows and sighed, "I promise, I'll call."

THE SHEEP THIEF

As Jean left Harvey's office, she said, "It's 2577. Call me Monday after you've talked with him. I want to know what he said."

Harvey told Jean good-bye, sat back and briefly thought about the last couple of hours and the story Jean had shared with him about the sheep thief and the saint. Jean really did seem to care. Harvey knew their friendship was genuine and would continue to grow no matter who had what job. He felt better just knowing their relationship had not suffered. He also felt better because he now had a little hope that someone was out there who could help him.

Then reality kicked back in and Harvey immediately remembered a phone conversation he'd had earlier in the day about sending some material out to one of his people and how he'd promised to get it in the mail before he went home. He started putting together the package of brochures and other pieces. As he was finishing up, he was startled by a light knock on his door. He turned to see an elderly gentleman with a smile on his face standing there. "I hate to bother you this late. I know you're busy and trying to get out of here. But I just ran into Jean Bennett as she was leaving the building. It sure was good to see her again. She told me about her new job, and then she told me about the two of you meeting just a little while ago. She said she had mentioned my name to you. I'm sure she probably told you about us working together as well."

"Yes, she did," Harvey said as he sealed the envelope.

"I really am proud of her." The old man said, "I've had the privilege of working with a lot of people over the years, and none of them needed less help from me than Jean. She had hit a few rough bumps in the road that caused her self-esteem to take a hit, but overall she had a lot going for her. About all I had to do was emotionally pick her up, give her a word of encouragement and send her on her way. She did the rest. Well, that's enough about Jean; she said you were going to call me Monday morning. So I decided I'd take a chance and drop by your office just to see if you were still here instead of waiting for you to call Monday."

Harvey said, "You must be Mr. Taylor," as they shook hands. Mr. Taylor then asked with a slight smile, "Do you have a minute?"

"So this is the guy who helped Jean," Harvey thought. Even though it was close to 6 p.m. and he was tired and in a hurry, Harvey felt like it was Christmas morning and Santa himself had just arrived. Mr. Taylor looked just like Jean had described him—well-tailored suit, white shirt, everything—including the gold monogrammed cuff links. They talked about the business, all that was going on at Millspring—how well the stock was doing, even in the face of all the incredible world events and the stock market. They discussed the projects Harvey was involved in and some of the challenges he was facing with a few of the people in his department. Then Mr. Taylor sat back and, with a smile that reminded Harvey of the smile he'd seen on Jean's face, said, "Jean told me you felt like bailing out and heading out on the highway to wherever it took you. Just like she wanted to do a few years ago." Harvey thought, "Who does Jean think she is, telling this guy—a member of the board—that I'm thinking about quitting, especially when she knows I didn't really mean it?" Harvey's hesitation and the look on his face caused Mr. Taylor to apparently realize he'd struck a nerve because he then quickly added, "I can tell from the conversation we've had and the way you've talked about Millspring that you're not going anywhere, though, but there *is* something else going on. What is it?"

Harvey relaxed and started talking. As he told Mr. Taylor his story, it seemed with every word he wanted to open up even more. He even told him how Jean had shared the legend of the sheep thief with him. Harvey noticed how both of Mr. Taylor's eyebrows jumped up as a smile spread across his face when Harvey mentioned the story.

"It seems like more people remember that story than anything else I tell them," commented Mr. Taylor.

When Harvey finished sharing everything, Mr. Taylor said, "I've heard similar stories. You're certainly not the first person to have those thoughts."

"I'm sure," Harvey said. Then he continued, "As a matter of fact, as you said, Mr. Taylor, you and I both know Jean had similar feelings not too long ago. Jean told me she owes all her success to you and that you are the one who really helped put her on the right path again. Think you can do anything for me?"

Mr. Taylor knew he could help. Over the years how many had he seen like Harvey. For a moment he found himself drifting back to what he had done to turn his own life around so long ago. How he had made a promise to help others. He started thinking about some of the ones he had worked with like Jean, but he caught himself and got back to Harvey…the one who was shaping up to be his next project. If Harvey only knew, that's why he'd showed up in the first place. Truth is, that was his job—helping people just like Harvey. But he didn't tell Harvey all of that.

He simply said, "Sure. I can help you," and he went on to say, "Harvey, you can see all this gray hair of mine and these wrinkles… They are the outward signs of experience, and my experience has enabled me to boil down everything I've done to help myself and others to thirty-one ideas I'll be sharing with you, Harvey. After each idea, we'll stop and discuss it thoroughly. We'll focus, above all, on understanding and actually *applying* the idea to your life. If you're serious about changing your life, pulling yourself out of the rut you're in and being prepared for future opportunities, I promise you our time together will be well spent. But you've got to agree to stick with it and not leave me physically or, more important, mentally until we finish all thirty-one of them. AND...you've got to agree to give every one of them an honest 'try'… Agreed?"

"Agreed," was all Harvey said as he half frowned and thought to himself, *"Thirty-one. Whatever happened to, say,* The 5 Steps to Success or 7 Habits or at worst, the 10 scrolls—but thirty-one? *Come on…"*

Mr. Taylor said, "Tomorrow's Saturday. I don't have anything pressing in the morning. How about meeting me here at 9:00 a.m.? It will be quiet—no phone interruptions and very few people. We can get started then. One other thing—you are right—thirty-one is a lot." Harvey glanced back quickly at Mr. Taylor, smiled and said, "You're the boss," while he wondered if this guy was some sort of mind reader.

Harvey almost immediately felt some of his old self surface as he thought, "Wait a minute, is he kidding me? Saturday? Here?" Luckily, before he could say anything, he remembered how he'd felt that morning and how he'd genuinely wanted some help, and now here was someone willing to do just that and he thought, "Why not?" and it was odd how that momentary change of heart enabled him to feel a level of excitement and anticipation he hadn't felt in years. He couldn't wait to get started with his newfound friend, especially a board member—you just never know when you might need a friend in high places. He thought for just a second more and remembered he didn't have his children this weekend, so without a second thought, Harvey said, "I'll be here… 9 a.m. sharp, and I'll even bring the donuts."

Mr. Taylor got up from his chair, walked toward the door and, with a smile on his face, said, "Great! I'll see you first thing in the morning."

Harvey just sat there for a few minutes thinking about all that had happened since this morning at 7:30 a.m. when he'd walked into his office…and here it was almost 7 p.m. He chuckled to himself as he flashed back to a conversation he'd had with Doc Henry sometime around the first week he'd started working with the company. Doc had called him into his office for the personal chat that Harvey later learned was part of the orientation all of the people who came to work at Wellspring Industries went through, and the only thing Harvey remembered about that conversation was Doc rearing back in his chair and saying, "Harvey, you're gonna love working here mainly because we only work half days around this place and you can pick any 12 hours you want." And then he let out a big laugh as he patted me on the back and welcomed me to the company. "I remember laughing at that comment," Harvey thought, but everyone learned Doc wasn't kidding. As he put the envelope he had to mail under his arm and hit the light switch on his way out, he thought, "One of these days, these 'half-days' are going to do me in."

CHAPTER IV
STAIRWAY TO THE STARS

Mr. Taylor started off the first session on Saturday morning with this story: "Some time ago on a flight out of Atlanta, the man sitting next to me began to tell me almost the same kind of story you told me yesterday, Harvey. Although this gentleman had worked hard to become successful, he hadn't succeeded. He shared all sorts of random thoughts and ideas, but without realizing it, near the end of our flight, he revealed the two main reasons why he was NOT a success. He looked at me and said, almost as if he were angry yet at the same time full of despair, 'You know, you'd think a guy like me with a good education and good work habits is bound to be successful, especially since it seems that most of the people in this country are lazy, inconsiderate, have a victim mentality and are always looking for a handout or an easy way out.'

"There it was—the answer to all his troubles in one sentence. He made it very clear that his attitude toward life and people was one of cynicism and negative expectancy. He saw the majority of people as being less than he thought he was. He saw them as 'second-rate' citizens. He was always looking for and finding the worst in people and in most situations. He was also working under the misconception that all you need to get ahead in life is a formal education and hard work. He apparently didn't know that out of the entire body of knowledge people acquire in a lifetime, only a small percentage comes from their formal education. Don't misunderstand me, Harvey, it is extremely important to get as much formal education as we can, but it does not come with a guarantee of success. What are you excited about, Harvey? What is the biggest thing you are trying to accomplish?"

Harvey laughed somewhat incredulously and shot back with, "If I can just keep getting up every morning, coming to work, getting my paycheck and make it to retirement, I'll be lucky." After what seemed like an eternity, Mr. Taylor asked, "Is that it? Nothing else turns your crank. There's nothing else you want to accomplish?" Harvey felt like he'd not given Mr. Taylor the answer he wanted. "I want to make a good life for my children, do things with them, help them get a good education—you know, stuff like that?" he said hesitantly.

Mr. Taylor seemed to shift mental gears and asked, "I wonder, Harvey, are you as tired as I am of the cynicism, arrogance and just plain old negative thinking I sometimes see in others like that guy on the plane?"

"I sure am," Harvey replied.

Mr. Taylor went on, "That guy was suffering from bland, weak and, most of the time, no ambition. He was surviving, not thriving, Harvey…and that is the same kind of thinking I just heard come out of your mouth. One of the most effective formulas for failure is arrogance and cynicism. Toss in a little despair, and you can speed up the downward spiral."

Harvey all of a sudden felt real self-conscious and a little uneasy with the response he'd given earlier. Harvey realized that he also felt a little cynical, down in the dumps, like he was headed down a dead-end street…and not just since the meeting yesterday morning but also since his divorce and since…wait a minute, he thought. How long had it been since he hadn't felt cynical and down in the dumps? Harvey remembered having just recently told someone that one of his biggest fears was that he would end up being like his daddy. Harvey had always seen his dad as the "king of the cynics." Nothing ever went right. His dad believed that whenever something bad happened it was always someone else's fault. Everybody was out to get you, and life in general was basically the pits. His dad's golden rule was, "Do unto others before they do unto you." Now, here he was, in the process of making his worst fear a reality. In his mind, he realized he was sounding just like his daddy.

Mr. Taylor smiled as he resumed. "You see, Harvey, we are all but guaranteed second-rate lives when we THINK second-rate thoughts about ourselves or others. The reason is that those thoughts cause us to SAY and DO second-rate things. Constantly judging others in a negative way is a second-rate way to think. When a person does that, they are not seeing people with their eyes, Harvey. They are seeing them with their hardened heart, their bruised ego and their poor set of values.

"For many years I have been interested in the subject of greatness and have tried to determine the common denominator in great and wonderful people—truly successful people. And I have discovered what I deeply believe are the specific keys to joy, wealth, feelings of significance and a totally renewed spirit. Not only have I discovered them through the study of successful people, but I've also learned them through personal trial and error. Also, five or seven won't do it. It takes all 31 working in harmony."

Mr. Taylor went on. "Back in my younger days, I made some poor choices. I even did some things I'm not proud of. But I've dealt with every one of them, and I've been moving onward and upward ever since. More important though, I've had the incredible privilege of helping so many young people like you. I want to pass these ideas on to you, Harvey. All 31 of them.

"But there's a catch. The ideas come one at a time, and before you can get the next idea you have to make sure the one you just received is working for you. In some cases, you'll realize that step is already a part of your life. If it is, just acknowledge it and move on to the next one. Just like in climbing, make sure you're standing solidly on one step, though, before you take the next one.

THE SHEEP THIEF

"Before I share these ideas with you, Harvey, I'd like you to do something. I want you to close your eyes and just relax for a moment. Take a couple of deep breaths; clear your head and picture a huge stairway. A grand set of steps made of granite that are several feet wide…8 to 10 feet wide. You are standing on the ground in front of the first step, and as you look up, you realize they extend so high that you can barely see the top…but you can see it and your eyes begin to focus on the highest step. Now I want you to visualize a locked door way up at the top of that magnificent stone stairway. The stone stairs aren't made from just any granite; these steps are made from smooth pink granite. Each step is highly polished to such luster that the top of each step looks almost wet. Picture yourself standing at the foot of that stairway. Can you see yourself there, Harvey?" Harvey, with closed eyes, slowly nodded his head. "Now I want you to let your eyes go over each step. There are over 30 steps in this grand stairway. Let your mind's eye see each one. The 31st step is through that door at the top of the stairs, and it is the most important step of all."

The room was quiet for a moment or two as Mr. Taylor gave Harvey time to visualize the stairway. Then he said, "Are you near the top?" Harvey nodded again. "As you near the top of the stairs you'll see the door I mentioned earlier. Right across the center of the door are four words. Those four words are in brass letters—**TRUE HAPPINESS AND SUCCESS**. As you look at the door, Harvey, you will notice something very unusual. Instead of being one door with the traditional one lock, this door has 30 locks. That's right. Thirty brass deadbolt locks. Logic tells you that if there are 30 locks, then they must all be unlocked before the door will open. But that's not the way this door works."

Then, he said, "In order for you to open the door, only a certain number of the locks have to be unlocked. In other words, you'll only have to put the special key that's waiting for you at the top of the stairs into the locks that need to be unlocked in your life. Those are the ones that will unlock the door to true happiness and success in your life. Only the combination that fits you will open the door for you. Someone else would need to unlock a different number of those locks for their door to open.

"The locks for the steps that are already a part of your life are open right now. All you have to do is unlock the ones that are not a part of Harvey Cole's life today."

"I'm not sure that I understand. Tell me again how I will know which locks will unlock the door?" Harvey asked as he opened his eyes.

"OK," Mr. Taylor said. "Close your eyes again, Harvey. Look at the door again. Now, work your way back down the steps, and as you do, I want you to imagine there are words written on the front of each step of the stairway. There may be a single word or even a phrase. None are distinguishable right now. Don't even try to read them. Just picture words on the front of steps. They're blurry now but that's OK. You'll only be able to read the words on one step at a time. And you'll only be able to read the next step once you realize you already possess the quality you are standing on or, through whatever amount of effort it takes, acquire the quality and make it a habit—an integral part of your life. In other words, as you stand on each step, you will have to decide if that idea is a part of your life right now or not. If it is, the next step will come into focus quickly and you'll be able to move up to it. When you get to the door, the locks that represent the steps with the words that are already a part of your life will be unlocked when you get there. Only those steps—those ideas that you aren't using now and need to put some effort into—will have to be opened. The ideas that are not a part of your life right now will make up your unique combination of locks that only you will know. And you'll know for sure if you've truly made a particular characteristic a part of your life because the lock will open easily once you put the key in it. However, if you have not mastered that characteristic, the lock won't budge and the door to **True Happiness and Success** will stay closed to you, Harvey."

Harvey opened his eyes and nodded as he said, "So only the steps I need to work on will unlock corresponding locks and open the door?"

"You got it," Mr. Taylor said with another of his now familiar smiles.

"When we do start this journey, there is no way in the world we can cover all of the ideas I want to share with you in one sitting. You can't just bound up these steps like a kid running to get into a candy store. Only after you've digested, internalized and are practicing each idea and feel you're ready to move on can we move to the next step. Once you feel you have a good handle on the ideas in our first session, then we can move to the next one. The pace will be completely up to you. When you are ready to move on, just call my extension 2577 and I'll come running. Your time is valuable, Harvey, so I don't want you taking the time to traipse up to my office to get past our gatekeeper, Margaret, or feel intimidated just because you're sitting in my overdecorated, overstuffed office. So, just call and we'll set a time to get together.

"One other thing. After we discuss an idea, I'll give you a worksheet with some affirmation statements on it about that step to help you implement it. Since I want you to work on the idea every day, each worksheet will have the words "Daily Statement" at the top of the page. You'll see a statement or maybe even several statements that I want you to repeat over and over in your head until they sink in. The statement will be followed by a place for you to write down the date you started working on that step. It will also have room for you to take notes so you can write down what you plan to do to make it a part of you and the benefits you derived. Kind of like a journal on each step. We'll keep all of those in a notebook that you'll build and keep nearby all the time as a constant reminder and as a rich resource of very useful information.

"I'm also going to recommend some books for you to read. I noticed you have a few books here in your office. Do you have any books anywhere else?"

"I have some at home," Harvey confidently replied because he didn't want Mr. Taylor to know the few he had were a decade or so old and collecting dust on the one bookshelf he had at home. Harvey had heard other people talking about some of the books they were reading, but he never seemed to have the time to just sit and read.

"Books are truly a treasure, Harvey. In addition to our work together I recommend you start by reading one book a month. I know you can't read all of them today, but you can start reading them today. What's that old saying, 'A journey of a thousand miles begins with one step'? Well, the reading of a thousand books begins with reading the first one.

"Here's a thought for you, Harvey. You are forty-five years old."

"Yes," Harvey replied as he wondered how Mr. Taylor knew that.

Mr. Taylor went on, "If you live to be ninety-five, that's fifty more years of living. If you start reading one book a month right now, by the end of your life you will have read only six hundred books plus what you've already read. Harvey, did you know that there are over 100 million items in the United States Library of Congress? We'd have to gather 166,667 people who would be willing to read one book a month for the next fifty years just to read everything they have as of today. That doesn't even count the vast number of new books that are published every year along with the ones that will be published over the next fifty years. Nor does it include all the works on medicine or agriculture because those writings are all housed in their own separate libraries."

"Wow, I'm behind in my reading already, aren't I?" Harvey laughed.

"Yes, but most of us are, Harvey, most of us are," Mr. Taylor said as his mind wandered back to some of the great books he'd read over these many, many years...and he'd read them all. Great books—classics—by such noted authors as Oswald Chambers, Ralph Waldo Emerson, Og Mandino, Napoleon Hill, Dr. Norman Vincent Peale, Charles "Tremendous" Jones, Dale Carnegie and so many others.

He realized he'd drifted off in thought as he was interrupted by Harvey, asking, "OK, when can we get started?"

"How about right now?" Mr. Taylor said as a big smile opened up all over his face.

CHAPTER V
LAYING THE FOUNDATION: THE ATTITUDE FACTOR

"By the way," Mr. Taylor asked Harvey, "Do you have a loose-leaf or a spiral notebook handy?"

"No," Harvey answered, "But I can get one."

Mr. Taylor stopped him. "That's okay. For now, just use a fresh legal pad. You'll want to punch some holes in the pages for your notebook we mentioned earlier, or if you'd prefer to take notes on your laptop, that's fine. You can save them in a folder or print them out later. Whatever you are more comfortable with, that works for me.

"Let's start with some observations about ourselves that have been tested by time. For instance, it has been said, 'Our main task as we grow older is to retain the capacity for the joy of discovery and to learn from our pupils as we teach *them* to see the possibilities in all things.'

"I refer to this as a sense of wonder, Harvey, and we'll talk more about it a little later. It is really central to all good things.

"Arnold Toynbee, the noted historian, has said the average age of the world's great civilizations has been 200 years. No more than the blink of an eyelash in the unfolding panorama of history. All nations, he says, have progressed through the following steps:

From bondage to spiritual faith
From spiritual faith to great courage
From courage to liberty
From liberty to abundance
From abundance to selfishness
From selfishness to complacency

From complacency to apathy
From apathy to dependency
From dependency back again to bondage

"The philosopher, Santayana, said, 'If we forget about our history, we are doomed to repeat it.' Wouldn't you agree that the majority of those words are simply attitudes?"

Harvey nodded as Mr. Taylor went on. "What that means to me then is that our ATTITUDES are truly conditioned by our history, and most of our history is conditioned by our ATTITUDES.

"Toynbee also wrote, 'Our destiny is NOT predetermined for us; we determine it for OURSELVES.' Again, our attitudes as individuals, as organizations and as nations determine our destiny.

"You see, it makes no difference whether you are short or tall, fat or thin, bald or hairy, male or female, or whether you are white, yellow, red, brown, tan or black. And trust me, I do not want to trivialize the part gender and race play, but none of those things matter near as much as your attitude. Attitudes are not only the ingredients for a solid foundation, they are the fuel you need for BECOMING more than you are right now. W. Clement Stone, the founder of Combined Insurance Companies of North America, said, 'There is very little difference in people, but that little difference makes a big difference. The little difference is attitude, and the big difference is whether or not it is positive or negative.'

"The importance of accepting WHO you really are is also critical. And, I quickly add, is not new. The only thing new is that many people are just now discovering the importance of being that unique and potentially splendid creation known as your BEST SELF and not trying to be like anyone else's best self. Perhaps the most splendid statement of being yourself was given to us by the God of the Universe when he said, 'I AM THAT I AM!' He *is* God. He created us. We are His children and are expected to be what He wants us to be—unique—possessing our own set of strengths and skills and knowledge and attitudes and gifts and talents. The only way we can honor those is to use them to the fullest and in the way they were intended to be used.

"Some of the world's greatest thinkers have made the following statements about the attitudes of 'self' that ensure success:

Plato said, "Before you can move the world you must first move YOURSELF."

Socrates said, "Above all KNOW thyself."

Shakespeare said, "To thine own self be True."

Marcus Aurelius said, "Above all CONTROL thyself."

Aristotle said, "Lose yourself in productive work, in a way of excellence."

Emerson said, "What you are thunders so loud, I can't hear what you're saying."

Epictetus said, "Men are disturbed not by things, but by the view which they take of them."

Gandhi said, "You will FIND yourself in service to your fellow man, your country and your GOD."

And Edwin Markham said,
"Ah, great it is to believe the dream
As we stand in youth by the starry Stream,
But a greater thing is to live life through

And say at the end, 'the dream is true.'"

And the most important statement of all,
Christ said, "Above all GIVE yourself away."

"In the coming years all of man's energies, dreams, joys, fears and strivings should focus on four things. They are: self-discovery, self-fulfillment, self-actualization and co-actualization, in that order. As nations, we will never be able to get along with each other until we come to grips with who we really are. These are the primary processes that will engross all individuals, organizations, families and nations. Regrettably, most people don't know why and how to make them happen."

Mr. Taylor sat straighter and continued intently, "Let me add: when you determine who you are and what YOU want, and DECIDE to go after it, you have made the most important decision in your life.

"I might add here, Harvey, that great countries are great because the great people in them have great expectations. If great people cease to expect greatness, great countries will cease to be great. We write our own destiny. We become what we EXPECT and then DO. When we know who and what we wish to BE, what our expectations of ourselves are, then we will find it relatively easy to know what to DO. There is real dignity in a human's 'Being' but even more dignity in a human 'Doing,' if they are doing the right thing and that which God put them on this earth to do. Most important of all, though, is to know that every ounce of our Being and Doing rests solidly on our attitudes, our perceptions and our outlook.

"So, if you clearly see that each step on the stairway is directly affected by your ATTITUDES, you are ready to commence the climb."

Mr. Taylor paused and Harvey nodded his head as he

mentally reviewed what he had heard so far. Then Harvey said, "You're saying we have to change our outlook about ourselves, about other people and about what we expect from the world around us. Is that the first step?"

"Yes, but it's not the first step of the staircase."

Harvey shook his head. "If you're trying to confuse me, you're succeeding."

"I'm not trying to confuse you, Harvey. I just want you to realize that undergirding every successful life is a successful attitude toward self, others and, above all, toward God. At this very moment, you are truly on the threshold of breathtaking new discoveries about human potential. Our attitude is the foundation, the platform on which we build everything else. No structure of any kind can survive a weak foundation. If you enter into our work together with an attitude of negative expectancy, that is, not expecting this to work for you, guess what—it won't. Enter into it though with an attitude of positive expectancy and again, guess what— it will work. As Zig Ziglar said in his book that I recommend you read, *See You at the Top*, 'It's not our *altitude* but our *attitude* that determines how far we get in life.'

"Now that our foundation is laid, we're ready for the first step on the stairway that will lead to opening the door to success and happiness in life.

"One last thought before we start," said Mr. Taylor. "Because there are so many ideas I want to share with you, I'm going to give each one to you as succinctly as I possibly can. It will then be up to you to delve more deeply into the ones you need to work on the most."

CHAPTER VI
THE FIRST STEPS: FAITH—BELIEVE THE DREAM

Step 1—You Become What You Value

Mr. Taylor said, "The first step is, YOU BECOME WHAT YOU VALUE. I also believe you tend to become what you think you are. What the human mind can conceive, human abilities have proven they can ACCOMPLISH! We can do and be that which we BELIEVE we can do and be." He went on, "Can we be everything there is to be, Harvey?

"Of course not," Mr. Taylor said, answering his own question. "If you are six feet five inches tall and weigh 290 pounds, would you ever really consider being a jockey who would one day ride in the Kentucky Derby? Of course not, and conversely, if you are five feet two inches tall and weigh 105 pounds soaking wet, would you seriously consider playing professional basketball in the NBA? Probably not.

"However, if you see yourself as a unique and potentially splendid creation of a loving God, this is precisely what you CAN and WILL become. If you see yourself as a second-rate loser, that is precisely what you CAN and WILL become…which will always be less than you are capable of becoming."

As Harvey nodded, Mr. Taylor said, "In other words, the quality of our inner life leads to abundance in the world around us. The kind of person you THINK you are is the kind of person you ARE and are in the process of becoming. It shapes and forms and affects all that you say and all that you do and determines 100 percent of what and who you ARE.

"What we believe, think and act upon are our values.

Our values determine how we see ourselves. With weak or unclear values, life becomes a meaningless series of attempts to put more food in your stomach, a bigger roof over your head and to provide yourself with more of the physical and material comforts of life. Values such as faith, hope and love are the real vitamins a person needs. Add values like gratitude, appreciation and respect for self and others, and it all starts to fuse into a unified whole. Harvey, opposites may attract but opposites cannot coexist… You simply cannot be happy and sad at the same time… You are one or the other. Other examples of values that cannot coexist are gratitude and ingratitude, confidence and fear, determination and laziness, and on and on."

Then Mr. Taylor asked, "What do you believe in, Harvey? What truths do you stand on? What do you value most? What are you not willing to compromise? What are your priorities? Your answers to these questions will tell me more about you than anything else, and if they aren't clear, your 'thinking' and your daily activities will be like the wind—constantly changing.

"Values are the fuel for our actions in life. The right values help us decide to do the right thing before we even reach the moment of decision. Values help us do the right thing when we don't have time to think about how we should respond to a particular situation. Clear, well-defined values can not only help us stay out of trouble, they help us lead others in the way they should go."

Mr. Taylor continued with, "Harvey, I wouldn't begin to tell you what your values should be. Values vary from culture to culture and country to country. Don't think for a minute I want to impose my values on you. My values are based on my beliefs and how I was socialized. My values have changed over the years. Early on in my life, part of my values said, 'If I see it, want it and you have it, it's OK for me to take it as long as I don't get caught.' Another one was,

'Always take the easy way out—if I can get it without working for it, great.' I paid a big price for acting out those values, Harvey.

"Have you ever heard of the Law of Cause and Effect? It says that for every action there is an equal and opposite reaction. Let me give you an example. A gentleman I worked with about ten years ago told me a story about how bad values caused him some emotional pain when he experienced the Law of Cause and Effect.

"He had been a Boy Scout, and his Scout troop used to camp in the mountains that were about a hundred miles from their hometown. Each summer they rode the community bus to the camp. His first year, they stopped at a little gift shop shortly before they arrived at the campsite. It was loaded with all sorts of trinkets. Now keep in mind, these were Boy Scouts who had each raised their right hand and pledged to be honorable. As I'm sure you remember, the pledge even starts off, 'On my honor…'

"As they entered the store, this young man remembered that one of the traditions in his family was that when his dad went away on a trip, he would bring back a gift for everyone in the family. He wanted to do the same thing, but he wanted the easy way out. He didn't want to spend his own money.

"Some of the older Scouts had been talking about how easy it would be to steal something from the store, so he thought that would be the solution. He could steal something for his mama, his daddy and his sister and little brother. He went through the store and found a little something for each of them and stuffed each one inside his shirt. The theft was a success. He felt a little twinge of guilt but not much. Plus he rationalized that since the rest of them were stealing it was perfectly all right for him to help himself to a few items.

"When he got back on the bus, he went to the back where all the gear was stored, found one of his bags and carefully stuffed his stash down in the bottom under everything else and forgot about it. They had a great week of camping, and the theft never crossed his mind again.

"On the return trip, about twenty miles before they got back to home base and their waiting families, he decided to check on his presents he planned to proudly give each of his loved ones the minute he stepped off the bus…just like his daddy always did. He went to the back of the bus, got the bag with the presents, opened it and put his hand down under his now dirty clothes to retrieve the gifts. He searched everywhere including his other bag, and they were nowhere to be found. He looked up to see several of his fellow Scouts looking back at him and laughing. A couple of them in unison even said, 'Lose something?' He knew instantly what had happened. One or more of his fellow Scouts had stolen his stolen presents. He told me he learned two things that day, Harvey. There is no honor among thieves and that he had a bad value system that needed fixing. He went on to tell me that it took one more event in his life to finally get him straightened out. By the time I started working with him, stealing—anything, anytime, anyplace for any reason was not one of his problems. He'd solved that issue long before I got to him. He was truly a man with unimpeachable integrity."

Finally, Mr. Taylor really dug in when he said, "Harvey, if you can't tell me what you believe in, I can't believe in you. Does that make sense?" Mr. Taylor asked that question because of Harvey's look of uncertainty. Harvey said, "Kind of."

"'Kind of' is not good enough, Harvey. If you're not clear about this, you won't be able to take another step," Mr. Taylor quickly replied.

As Harvey quietly sat there, he realized his beliefs weren't clear. As he'd said the words "kind of," he realized they were not nearly as well defined as he suspected Mr.

Taylor wanted them to be. He thought about how he lived his life; his attitudes, actions, hopes and hurts; some of the plans he'd once had; what he'd accomplished, and what he hadn't accomplished, and he began to see how his values had played themselves out in the way he lived, but he also knew—for the first time—that because he'd never thought about it, much less written values down, he was kind of like a log floating in the water… Whichever way the tide or the currents were running, that's the way he went. He knew he had a pretty good set of beliefs; he knew right from wrong; he knew what it meant to be honest…or dishonest; he knew what the pangs of guilt felt like when he'd done the wrong thing, and he also knew how good it felt when he did the right thing. It was painfully obvious he needed to clarify his values before he could go any further. He knew he was basically a good person and he kind of knew what was important but...maybe his priorities had gotten out of whack. He made a note to go to work outlining, prioritizing and defining his values as soon as they finished this session.

Mr. Taylor could tell Harvey was doing a little thinking, so he waited a few seconds, then said, "As we continue, Harvey, I'll be assuming you KNOW that everything we DO and BECOME is a result of what we BELIEVE. Agreed?"

Harvey smiled sheepishly. "Yes, I agree. I have some work to do, don't I? I guess I'm just not sure how to get started." That all-knowing, confident look came across Mr. Taylor's face as he said, "I'll tell you exactly what to do to get started… Write this down.

"The first thing I want you to do is pretend you are at a head table in a huge banquet hall, all dressed up, as are the couple of hundred or so other people in the room, and you look back over your shoulder at a huge banner that stretches across the wall there at the front of the room. The white banner is about twenty feet long, five feet high and the huge red letters you see read CONGRATULATIONS HARVEY!

You are the guest of honor. It is your retirement banquet. The chairman of the board at Wellspring Industries welcomes everyone, dinner is served, you hear lots of chatter, and finally the chairman stands behind the lectern, quiets the crowd and introduces the first speaker, who is proceeded by several more people at Wellspring. They all stand up and talk about the kind of job you did, the kind of person you were, the kind of influence you had on others, the successes you had and a few of the more humorous missteps you had along the way. If that banquet were held tonight, Harvey, what would they say?"

Harvey thought back over just this day alone and how he'd acted, what he had said, what he had not said and wondered if based just on today…would anyone even show up for the banquet. Harvey lied and said, "I don't know." Well, it wasn't a total lie, he thought. But in his heart he knew that when he stacked today up with all the days that made up the past, it might not be the most enjoyable banquet he'd ever attended.

"Want to change the outcome?"

"Sure," Harvey shot back a little too quickly.

"OK, write out their speeches for them."

"What?"

Mr. Taylor repeated himself, "Write out their speeches for them. Write down what you would like them to say about the kind of employee, leader, friend, confidant, encourager and difference maker you were. Then you will have a target that has the potential…key word there, Harvey…potential…to influence how you live your life."

He went on. "Once you've written those out and set them aside, I want you to pretend it's…oh, say…thirty or so years later. You have had an incredible retirement—traveled the world, fished, played golf and whatever else you enjoy doing. Then, one day, without any warning you drop dead…no illness or pain…you simply die. A few days later, your family is all gathered around. For the purposes of this exercise, Harvey, I want you to bring all your immediate family together, even the ones who predeceased you. There in the funeral home are your spouse, your mom and dad, your siblings, your children and your grandchildren. You can hear them. Write down what you would like for them to say about the kind of husband, son, brother, father and grandfather you were. See where I'm going here, Harvey?" The same time Harvey's nodding and writing Mr. Taylor says, "And just like the retirement speech, what you write down has the potential...key word there again, Harvey...potential...to influence how you live your life.

"Finally, I want you to mentally move ahead ten more years. There are four people seated around a table in a restaurant. One is the best friend, outside of your spouse or another family member, that you had when you were living. The other is a neighbor you knew well...and you may have to go all the way back to your childhood to find one of those, since most people don't know their neighbors at all these days. The third is a friendly peer you had at Wellspring Industries and the last one is someone who was a fellow member of yours in a church, civic club or some other community organization.

"The four of them are drinking coffee and talking. One of them says, 'It is hard for me to believe that Harvey has been dead for ten years.' And the others nod in agreement as another one says, 'He was a great guy, and one of the things I really liked about him was...' and, Harvey, that's where you start writing. Fill in the blank for the comments made by each one of them that are what you would like for them to say about you, ten years after you are dead and gone."

Harvey's pencil is almost smoking he's writing so fast, as Mr. Taylor says again, "And just like the retirement speech and the funeral home family gathering, what you write down has the potential...key word there one more time, Harvey…potential…to influence how you live your life.

"Once you've written your thoughts down in those three main 'life arenas,' Harvey, I then want you to get out eight pieces of paper and write the word SPIRITUAL at the top of the first page; then at the top of the second page write the word FAMILY, then at the top of each of the rest of the pages, write PERSONAL GROWTH, HEALTH, PROFESSIONAL, FINANCIAL, COMMUNITY, and finally SOCIAL/RECREATIONAL.

"Now, go back to the retirement, funeral and ten-years-later notes, and based on what you would like to have said in each of those situations, write out what you believe…your values…on each of the titled pages. Write them in present-tense language, Harvey, and to do that, start with words like 'I believe…' or 'I am…' The tendency is to write your thoughts down like goals…in future tense. These are not goals. They are what you believe… They are the basis for goals and decisions… They are your values."

They both sat in silence as Harvey let all that he'd just heard roll around in his head. Mr. Taylor had been at this point with so many other people over the years that he knew the best thing he could do right now is to be quiet for as long as it took for Harvey to process everything.

As Harvey finally looked up at Mr. Taylor, he heard, "One other thought, Harvey—it takes some time but if you follow this proven process, it's fairly easy to work through and write down your beliefs, values, etc. Here's what is really important…and I picked this thought up in a book by Rick Warren titled *Purpose-Driven Life*—no matter how much you write down on a piece of paper about seeing yourself as honest, loving, faithful, brave, courteous, kind..." A smile came across Harvey's face, and Mr. Taylor stopped and said, "Sounds like we're back in Scouts, doesn't it?"

Harvey chuckled and said, "You're reading my mind."

Mr. Taylor smiled back and went on, "Obedient, reverent...and any other good word you can think of, the truth is, they are all just words on paper. We get to find out how faithful you are only when you have an opportunity to be unfaithful; we get to find out how honest you are when you have the chance to be dishonest; we get to find out how courteous you are when you have the chance to be discourteous or rude; we only get the chance to find out how reverent you are..."

Harvey interrupted with, "When I have a chance to be irreverent. I understand."

Mr. Taylor added, "Great success will only come when you can clearly define the basic beliefs that add energy, direction and meaning to your life. The total value of your mind is the product of your individual values."

Harvey realized that the first step on his journey to success and happiness required him to write out his values in clear, present-tense language, not future tense, as he thought to himself, "I will write a values statement (minimum 2 to 3 sentences) for every area of my life. Each one will start with the words 'I believe' or 'I am.' Harvey started making some notes about his spiritual values and wrote, "I believe in John 3:16. I also believe that God wants me to grow in my knowledge of Him and in my love for Him. I live every day as an example for others and as a witness for God"—he knew he could add more later.

While Harvey was writing, Mr. Taylor pulled a piece of paper out of a file folder he had with him and handed it to Harvey as he continued. "We can stop right now so you can go to work on this first step or we can move to the next step. Which would you prefer?"

"Let's move on," Harvey replied.

"Only under the condition that you'll spend time on and complete this first step before we get back together."

"I promise," Harvey said.

DAILY STATEMENT
TO HELP ME MASTER STEP #1
YOU BECOME WHAT YOU VALUE

I constantly seek to clarify my values. I know what values are important to me. I know what I stand for, what I believe in and what I will not compromise. I have written them out in present-tense language for every area of my life, and I review them regularly.

STEP 2—YOU BECOME WHAT YOU SAY

"The next step on this stairway to spiritual, financial and mental richness is the understanding that YOU BECOME WHAT YOU REPEATEDLY SAY. In recent years we have allowed a lot of meaningless words to creep into our vocabulary, even gutter language. How many times have you heard others say, 'I'd really be in trouble if my old English teacher were here and heard what I just said.' We're using too many lukewarm words. Ask the next ten people you meet how they're doing. You'll hear, 'Oh, I'm OK' or they'll hold their hand in front of themselves, waggle it from side to side, and say 'about 50/50.' What does that mean? Fifty percent of the time they're doing well and the other 50 percent of the time they're doing badly? Another I've yet to understand is 'fair to middlin.'

"TV has spawned an endless stream of nitty-gritty, mechanistic words, sound bites that are often negative, judgmental and mean-spirited. Viewers and listeners by the millions would gain new mental vitamins, new images and new hope if what was said was more positive and upbeat. The macho-direct approach to communications we hear today has also made many people afraid to use words denoting beauty, love and joy. It's 'safer' and less vulnerable to use tepid, tasteless words. Texting, tweeting, plaxoing, instant messaging, etc. have caused us to be brief, blunt and sometimes even brusque."

Mr. Taylor added, "A gentleman named Dr. Herman Kahn, the highly respected scientist and futurist, once said in a speech at the White House that the future could be 'glorious.' Yes, sir! 'GLORIOUS!!' That's the word he used. It is certainly a word we haven't heard very often these days, have we, Harvey? Why not?"

Mr. Taylor paused to let Harvey think about this for a minute, then again proceeded to answer his own question.

"Because WE TRULY DO BECOME WHAT WE REPEATEDLY SAY. When we have thoughts and use words which are great, we have no recourse but to become great people. The thought of living up to the greatness of our potential can be frightening, letting fear creep into our subconscious mind when we are both awake and asleep. Automatically, then, we begin to back away and use pale, listless, gritty and non-juicy words.

"If you consistently think of and use words like GLORIOUS and mean them, then glorious things happen to you. It's one of the great universal laws! Words can be blunt tools that bruise and abrade, or they can be potentially exquisite instruments, which create beauty and truth. So I challenge you, Harvey, to select and use ALL words as exquisite instruments for growth and success. Just be more conscious of the descriptive words you use.

"For example, learn to relish how these words make you feel as you use them: truth, strength, love, joy, excellence, vigor, tenderness, courage, fitness, peace, zest, sparkle and beauty."

Harvey noticed Seth Taylor's face became brighter as he said these words, and they did make him feel warm, strengthened and invigorated. Mr. Taylor resumed, "Wisdom is the perfect blending of experience, intelligence and love. And real wisdom comes only when we experiment and work at widespread and consistent USE of intelligence and love through WORDS, and make no mistake about it, Harvey, YOU REALLY DO BECOME WHAT YOU REPEATEDLY SAY!

"The great writer C. S. Lewis illustrates this principle in his writings. In the year after he had published the famous book called *The Screwtape Letters*, which are letters from the Devil, Uncle Screwtape, to his nephew on earth whose name was Wormwood, Lewis became mentally ill. These letters were written with an almost magic talent for subtle evil, vindictiveness and all of the lowest and basest emotions, with some perfect prescriptions from Uncle Screwtape to Wormwood on how to destroy all that was good and light and bright and wholesome on earth. The book sold hundreds of thousands of copies, the film made from it brought in a great amount of money, and C. S. Lewis became a financially wealthy man. But he later wrote that he was mentally ill for months because in the writings of that book he had first THOUGHT and then WRITTEN and then SPOKEN the kinds of words which he said left his mind 'full of itch, scratch and rot.' For months, even as the money poured in, he not only didn't feel good, he felt BAD! Then he decided he would use the same tools, the same instruments that he had used when he descended into those depths of spiritual decay and despair, to change his life, to turn around. And he wrote *Miracles*, *Peralandra* and *The Chronicles of Narnia* series for children. These books were full of beautiful imagery and beautiful experiences, wonderful discoveries and delicious tastes, both on this planet and in faraway and beautifully conceived parts of the universe. He wrote much about a place he called 'deep heaven.' He became well, and finally successful as a vibrant and whole human being." Best of all, millions have seen and hopefully have been positively influenced by the movies made from

The Chronicles of Narnia series and other words that came from C. S. Lewis."

Mr. Taylor paused, giving Harvey a chance to assess these demonstrations of the power of words. Harvey nodded his head after a few moments of thought, and Mr. Taylor pulled out a second sheet of paper for Harvey to add to his notebook. As he handed it to Harvey, he hesitated as if deep in thought. Then he said, "Studies have shown that profanity almost always preceded a physical outburst. Think about that next time you hear someone mutter a cuss word.

"One of the hardest habits to break is to stop saying the profanity some people utter every time they get mad or even just a little irritated."

Harvey thought, "He probably doesn't want to hear my choice words that always seem to make a stuck drawer or a door open, a lawnmower or a weed eater crank or an aggravating key turn in a lock." But what came out of Harvey's mouth was, "You are right. Seems like I always have a verbal outburst right before I bear down on whatever inanimate object is not doing what I want it to do or working the way I think it ought to work. You're saying that is contributing to my state of mind?"

"I sure am," Mr. Taylor said. "It's all about controlling your emotional outbursts. Have you ever thought about how silly it is to think that verbally laying a 'blue streak' of every word of profanity you've ever learned on an object is going to make any difference at all?" Harvey laughed and nodded, but didn't say a word. He knew he had no defense because he was guilty. He'd caught himself several times when he was in the car with his girls, shouting some obscenity to someone who had done something he thought was stupid, only to feel embarrassed when he realized what a bad influence that was on them. "That's got to stop," he thought.

DAILY STATEMENT
TO HELP ME MASTER STEP #2
YOU BECOME WHAT YOU SAY

I know and believe that the words I repeatedly use have an impact on who I am. I will use only words that are helpful (not hurtful), positive (not negative), encouraging (not discouraging) and tasteful (not distasteful).

STEP 3—BUILD ON STRENGTHS

"The third great step on the stairway to joy and renewal is to BUILD ON STRENGTHS. First, we must see what a weakness is. Give me a definition."

Harvey then chimed in, "A weakness is the inability to do something."

Mr. Taylor then said, "Close. What is the opposite of the inability to do something?"

Harvey said, "Well, I guess it would be the ability to do something."

"Exactly," said Mr. Taylor. He went on, "Can we call the ability to do something a strength?"

Harvey said, "Well, yes."

Mr. Taylor then smiled and said, "So now we can say that a weakness is simply the absence of a strength. Agreed?"

Harvey smiled and said, "That makes sense."

Harvey repeated slowly, "A weakness is the ABSENCE of a strength? I always thought knowing your weakness was supposed to be important and that was what we were supposed to focus on. Now that I realize it's really just an ABSENCE of something good, that changes the entire picture."

Mr. Taylor went on. "You're right again, that's all it is. A weakness is simply a zero, a minus, a vacuum. A LACK, something that's either missing or insufficiently developed.

It indicates we NEED something, and that SOMETHING we need will always be a strength, not another weakness. The majority of human beings have spent very little time to discover their own STRENGTHS, much less identifying strengths in others! Most of mankind has dissipated much of its potential through an entirely unnecessary amount of concentration on weaknesses.

"We are defined and profiled by our strengths. Our weaknesses only help us determine what additional strengths we need. The only valid reason for identifying a person's weaknesses is to determine what additional strengths are needed for successful results. If we dwell on each other's weaknesses, we'll never truly get to KNOW one another. Our strengths are what we ARE. Weakness should only be identified in order to determine (a) what additional strengths are needed or (b) what is needed to further develop existing strengths. I would challenge ANYONE to give me one other basic reason for being concerned about weaknesses.

"If we dwell on and agonize over our own inadequacies, we cannot see our strengths. And when we cannot see strengths in ourselves, we cannot see them in other people. Life is like a mirror which gives back to each of us the reflection we see of ourselves. We are imprisoned by our weaknesses. We are liberated by our strengths.

"I expect almost everyone recalls the statement, 'pride goeth before a fall'—well, so does a life focused solely on the weaknesses in others in some attempt to make oneself either look or feel superior. Dwelling on weaknesses is not only the gutless and expedient path, but also the path of the insecure and unenlightened person. Such people overcompensate for their own insecurities by appearing conceited, selfish, egotistical and self-centered.

"Actually, this seeming arrogance is a screen for the lack of a deep, sustaining self-confidence. Real self-confidence becomes possible only by an adequate and, eventually even a SPLENDID, awareness of present and potential STRENGTHS. The most scarce ingredient in daily living and in business today is deep, sustaining self-confidence. Again, it is the quintessential liberator.

"So, Harvey, what are your strengths? Identify them and then spend all your energy applying them. You can start by making a list of 25 strengths you see in yourself."

"Are you kidding me? Twenty-five strengths? I can think of four or five…but 25?" Harvey exclaimed.

"Just get started. If I'm any judge of character at all, once you get started, your ego will kick in and you'll come up with 50," and they both laughed.

"Are you ready to continue, Harvey? Have you absorbed the ideas on the steps we've climbed so far? Do you need to stop now? Do you want to plan another session for later?"

Excited by what he was hearing, Harvey started to nod "yes" but ended up by shaking his head "no." Chuckling out loud at his confusion, he said, "I'm sorry, please continue!" as Mr. Taylor handed him his third worksheet to add to his growing collection.

DAILY STATEMENT
TO HELP ME MASTER STEP #3
BUILD ON STRENGTHS

I will pursue greater knowledge of my strengths for the rest of my life. I will maximize strengths and minimize weaknesses in myself and everyone I meet. I have written out my strengths and review them regularly.

STEP 4—ATTEMPT THE DIFFICULT

Mr. Taylor smiled. "OK, Harvey, on we go. The next step up this stairway is supported by a famous behavioral scientist. Forty years ago, the eminent psychologist, Dr. Henry Link, said that, based on very extensive research, the one common denominator in the lives of ALL HAPPY people was that virtually every day such men, women and children either did, or attempted to do, something DIFFICULT. But, WE ONLY HAVE THE CONFIDENCE TO KEEP ATTEMPTING THE DIFFICULT IF WE START OFF DETERMINED TO RESPECT AND BELIEVE IN OURSELVES AND OUR ABILITY TO ACCOMPLISH THE DIFFICULT!! When we pursue a challenging path, we grow and renew at an exponential rate!

"History has shown us that the most incredible thoughts, words and deeds are almost always preceded by obstacles, adversities and tragedies. No truly successful person ever became successful without doing a great many things she or he feared to do, but had the courage to do in spite of fear. Unless we concede that we can fail and that failure doesn't mean total destruction of self, we will never be able to achieve success and happiness.

"To remove the fear of failure, refuse to let your mistakes harness you. Learn from every mistake you make and try not to make the same mistake twice. Make your decisions and forget them, then go on. Fail forward!

"Thomas Alva Edison, the inventor of the lightbulb, came up with thousands of ways that wouldn't work before around midnight one evening, he discovered the way to make it work. Then the first words he heard were from Mrs. Edison when she said, 'Tom, turn out that light and come to bed.' OK, maybe that second part isn't true, but we do know Dr. Edison failed a lot before he succeeded.

"Babe Ruth, Mickey Mantle, Hank Aaron, Willie Mays, Ken Griffey Jr., Reggie Jackson, and Alex Rodriguez all struck out more times at bat than they hit home runs, but the home runs are what we remember them for because they didn't quit when they did strike out.

"The old saying, 'It is always darkest before the dawn,' is almost always true. I say almost because there have been some incredibly successful people who, I'm sure, succeeded almost immediately. However, I doubt their success was anywhere near as sweet as it was for those who had failed before they succeeded. Have you ever worked out in your yard all day, Harvey, gotten a lot done and at the end of the day you were filthy dirty?"

"Yes, sir, I sure have."

"You know how good it feels when you step out of the shower later that evening?" Mr. Taylor kind of half asked and half told Harvey.

"I certainly do," said Harvey.

"You had to get a little dirt on you to make you really appreciate being clean. That is how those folks who have endured some hardships must feel. We can't let the fear of getting a little worn down, or a little dirty or of the unknown hold us back, Harvey.

"Life is too short to waste precious moments in fear of nothing. Once we have confronted fear, looked at it squarely, we'll discover that the only thing we feared was the fear that we would be fearful. I'm starting to sound like Franklin Delano Roosevelt when he said to the citizens of the United States of America at the height of the Depression, 'The only thing we have to fear is fear itself.'

"Individuals need to do what one of the greatest countries the world has ever known did when faced with the Great Depression. We need to yank ourselves up by our bootstraps, look fear square in the face and take one giant step forward.

"Now, Harvey, we can only take this fourth step and continue toward the door of success and self-actualization when we continue to reach for difficult goals which require us to DIG DEEP into our own mental and spiritual reservoirs and constantly bring new strengths to the surface. In this process, then, we continue to DISCOVER AND BUILD new strengths.

"The study of ourselves is like the search for diamonds in South Africa. People found a few diamonds in yellow clay and were delighted with their good fortune. They thought that this was the full extent of their find. THEN, they dug deeper and came to blue clay. To their amazement, they found in the blue clay as many precious stones in a day as they had previously found in a year. What had formerly seemed like wealth faded into insignificance beside the new riches. Don't stop at the yellow clay!!! PRESS ON to the rich, blue clay and the even greater riches beyond your present concept of self. Keep reaching continuously for new possibilities! Here's a copy of a poem I discovered a few years ago. It has reinforced Step #4 for many people. Maybe it will help you, as we face the difficulties of life."

PERSISTENCE

Two little young frogs from inland bogs
Had spent the night in drinking.
When morning broke, they both awoke
With eyes bloodshot and blinking.

'Fore time was had to gather senses
And breathe a prayer for past offenses,
A farmer frail came to the swale
And caught them quick as winking.

Now the farmer was a guileless man;
So he put the frogs in a big milk can.
But the can filled up and the lid came down;
Both frogs and milk were shipped to town.

Our friends began to shiver and quake
And sober up on a cold milk shake.

For now they had to kick and swim
Until their bleary eyes grew dim.

At last, one frog cried out in dread,
"We're gonna drown! We're good as dead!"
"For shame! For shame!" the other replied.
"A frog's not dead until he's died."

"Keep on kicking! That's my plan.
We may yet see outside the can."
"No use! No use!" faint-heart replied.
And with a groan he quickly died.

But the other frog, undaunted still,
Kept on kicking with a firmer will
Until with joy too great to utter,
He found he'd churned a lump of butter.
And hopping up on top of the grease
He floated around with the greatest of ease.

Now the moral of the story is:
When things are tough all over town,
Don't give up and don't go down.
Just keep on kicking; don't cry or mutter.
'Cause one more kick may bring your butter!

Author unknown

"Let's go back for a moment to Dr. Link, Harvey. His team of researchers dug deeply into attitudes, lifestyles and present levels of happiness. They studied the rich, the poor and those in between. They studied some ten thousand people! They found that a tragically large number of people really believed that happiness could be gained and retained totally by the pursuit of ease, escape, 'safeness' and expedience. When they went after life with that approach, what they found was that these people built up ever increasing feelings of guilt and self-loathing, two attitudes that are deadly enemies of real happiness. Thus, the accepted conclusion is that tranquility as an all-consuming goal is a quick consignment to oblivion.

"Shakespeare obviously knew the secret to living well when he wrote, 'Sweet are the uses of adversity.' There is something about taking on a tough and difficult challenge and having to work diligently to achieve it which burns away accumulated layers of guilt and self-disgust, and frees you up to really LIVE! Here, take this fourth page. Do you want to stop?"

"No, sir, let's keep going."

DAILY STATEMENT
TO HELP ME MASTER STEP #4
ATTEMPT THE DIFFICULT

I will continue to challenge myself to try new things in order to grow. I will relish living in the arena, not in the grandstand. I will fail forward!

STEP 5—WORK CONSCIENTIOUSLY AND PRODUCTIVELY

Mr. Taylor said, "Step five is: You must work conscientiously and productively. It is essential for mental and emotional health. Dr. Link's research has shown that a major common denominator in a long, healthy and happy life is putting in a lot of effort that is focused on clear, specific and stretching goals. You cannot take more OUT of life than you put IN. People who have little to do become tired because they tire of their own company and life becomes filled with imaginary shadows. You will also find life is more enjoyable when you are energetically progressing toward the accomplishment of something important.

"Early in my life I looked for shortcuts, Harvey. Don't misunderstand me, I believe in expediency, but not at the expense of quality. I don't believe in sacrificing thoroughness just because I'm not willing to work at something and see it through. All my life I've heard such things as, 'If you don't have time to do it right, when are you going to have time to do it over?' or 'You got to do it right the first time.'

"I also believe having a plan is critical. The only thing Don Quixote lacked was a practical plan of action. The best advice I can give for planning is to be very clear about the end results you want to see. Know what you want to accomplish, and then just simply work your way backward through all the steps necessary to make it happen and BEGIN.

"Those first steps may not seem as majestic as the end result will be, but they must be done in order to get where you want to go. Socrates said, 'Before we can do the noble, we must first do the useful.'

"I've been around hard-working people all my life, Harvey." With a laugh in his voice, Mr. Taylor went on, "I remember one of my earliest employers telling me the first day I went to work for him. He said, 'Hard work never killed anyone.' I'm not sure that's totally true, but he did teach about how to get more done than any person I've ever known.

"Harvey, as I built my businesses, I knew there were people in the world who were smarter than me, more talented than me and, in a few cases, better looking than me"—they both smiled—"yet I always believed no one could outwork me. I knew what I wanted to do and was willing to expend whatever amount of time, energy and talents I had to make that a reality. The next step…"

Harvey interrupted with, "What about the worksheet?"

Mr. Taylor chuckled again and said, "Hold on. We are

going to take this step and the next nine fairly quickly, so stay with me.

"In order to make this a little easier, here are the worksheets for each one. You just be sure and put the right one behind your notes for each step as I give them to you.

"Let's step up the pace a little. This next step is one of my favorites."

DAILY STATEMENT
TO HELP ME MASTER STEP #5
WORK CONSCIENTIOUSLY & PRODUCTIVELY

I am committed to the belief that working diligently pays off. I will do as Aristotle suggested when he said, "Lose yourself in productive work in a way of EXCELLENCE."

STEP 6—LAUGH OFTEN

"Have you ever known people who always went around with a sad, tired, depressed look on their face, Harvey? They are the kind of people that you are almost scared to ask, 'How ya' doing?' because you know whatever they say will be negative. I can't believe those people wouldn't want to be happy if they could. I know God wants us to be joyful and joyous in everything we do. He wants you to let your enjoyment of life show in laughter and joy. It really is wonderful medicine.

"Norman Cousins in his best-selling book *Anatomy of an Illness* proved there is an endorphin release that occurs when we laugh real hard. You know how when you laugh so hard you feel like you can't stop laughing or even catch your breath? You sometimes have maybe even laughed so hard that you felt lightheaded? That is when the endorphin release occurs. It is what runners call a runners' high. He even went on to say that laughter was internal jogging." Mr.

Taylor chuckled as he said, "Matter of fact, that's how I get my running in now, Harvey. It beats getting all sweaty and odiferous, doesn't it?

"Medical science has proven that endorphins are nature's healers that we can release anytime we want to with laughter. Plus it is the easiest medicine in the world to spread around, and on top of all that, it is free. Laughter truly is infectious. We need to help it become an epidemic! Though we travel the entire world over to find JOY, we must CARRY IT WITH US or we will never find it at all.

"That great philosopher and country comedienne Minnie Pearl once said, 'Laughter is God's hands on the shoulders of a troubled world.' It's true, Harvey. Laughter is a gift from God. I like to refer to it as our seventh sense. In school, we all learned the five senses: sight, touch, taste, smell and hearing. We often refer to our gut feelings as our sixth sense. I believe we also have a seventh sense—a sense of humor. Look for the laughter in life, Harvey. It's all around you. That's why I like to tell the story of the two little frogs I quoted earlier. It contains great truth, and it makes people laugh when they hear it.

"Here's a quote from Bob Murphy, an insightful, intelligent humorist from Nacogdoches, Texas. He says, 'Anybody who can get up in the morning, look in the mirror and get a good laugh out of what they see is gonna make it,' and I agree wholeheartedly with him, Harvey. King Solomon in Proverbs 17:22 said, 'A merry heart doeth good like a medicine.'

"That is my prescription for you, Harvey. I want you to laugh more. It doesn't take away from the seriousness of life or imply you take the challenges of life too lightly. What it does mean is that you have the confidence to laugh when something is funny. It means you are observant enough to see and enjoy the funny things that happen all around us. Don't you enjoy being with Jean and her family?"

"I sure do," Harvey replied.

"Why?" asked Mr. Taylor.

Harvey thought a minute. Then as a smile came across his face, he said, "There are a lot of reasons, but one is, they make me laugh."

As Harvey pondered that thought, Mr. Taylor handed him another piece of paper as he said, "Find a humorous book or a book on laughter. Then start out by writing down at least one funny thing you see, hear or read each day for the next week."

DAILY STATEMENT
TO HELP ME MASTER STEP #6
LAUGH OFTEN

I will find something to laugh about every day of my life. I will share this gift generously and often. I will start each day with a smile in my heart, knowing that the rest of my body will follow.

STEP 7—SELF DISCIPLINE

"Self-discipline is another must. As you look up to the top of the stairs of the successful life, you need to know your own critical path up those stairs. You need a blueprint—a map so that you are always striving toward a bright, clear beacon, which beckons and draws you. Great people train themselves to SEIZE, SHAPE and MASTER opportunity. Longfellow wrote, 'The heights by great men reached and kept WERE NOT ATTAINED BY SUDDEN FLIGHT, but they, while their companions slept, were turning upward in the night.'"

Mr. Taylor then added, "I don't know of one genuinely successful person anywhere who wasn't steadfastly disciplined about doing the things they had to do in order to get where they wanted to go. All the 'greats' will tell you that time after time they tired of doing the same thing over and over again, but each time they renewed their resolve, gritted their teeth and ran one more wind sprint, practiced the piano one more hour, made just one more sales call, wrote one more page or stayed just a little longer to prepare for tomorrow's presentation. They knew it would be easier to just stop and go do something that was a lot more fun or put off what they knew they should be doing until later, but they were willing to overcome laziness and delay today's small gratifications for tomorrow's greater prize.

"Everyone has to make a decision as to whether or not the goal they want to achieve is worth the effort they will need to expend to accomplish it. Most people seem to be satisfied with putting forth mediocre effort, which pretty much guarantees mediocre results…enough to get by but not enough to accumulate much extra, enough to keep from being fired but never promoted, enough to show up but not enough to get involved. Remember the old saying, 'You get what you pay for'?"

"I sure do," Harvey said.

"The same thing applies to life. What you get out of life will be in direct proportion to your effort. That's self-discipline. The willingness to do a little more, stay a little longer and fight a little harder. Malcolm Caldwell, in his book *Outliers: The Story of Success*, referred to a study conducted in the early 1990s by psychologist K. Anders Ericsson and two colleagues at Berlin's elite Academy of Music and said, 'The striking thing about Ericsson's study is that he and his colleagues couldn't find any "naturals," musicians who floated effortlessly to the top while practicing a fraction of the time their peers did. Nor could they find any "grinds," people who worked harder than anyone else, yet just didn't have what it takes to break the top ranks. Their research suggests that once a musician has enough ability to get into a top music school, the thing that distinguishes one performer from another is how hard he or she practices. That's it. And what's more, the people at the very top don't practice just longer or even much longer than everyone else. They practice much, much longer.' Caldwell also quotes neurologist Daniel Levitin, who said, 'The emerging picture from such studies is that ten thousand hours of practice is required to achieve the level of mastery associated with being a world-class expert in anything.'

"George Leonard, in his book, *The Art of Mastery*, uses an old martial arts quote that says, 'The master is the one who stays on the mat five minutes longer every day than anybody else.' He said practice is not something you do, but something you have or are… The people we know as masters don't devote themselves to their particular skill just to get better at it. The truth is, they love to practice.

"One of the most inspiring movies ever made was about the life of a young man who wanted to play football at Notre Dame more than anything else in the world. The only problem was he wasn't big enough or fast enough or mean enough to make it as a big-time college football player. However, his effort on the practice field so inspired the other players that when the coach wanted to deny him an opportunity to play in a regulation game, the other players brought their jerseys in one at a time to the coach's office and lay them on his desk, one on top of the other. Their message was clear. If Rudy is denied, we all will be denied. Have you ever seen the movie titled simply *Rudy*?"

"No, but I have a feeling I'm going to," Harvey said with a grin.

"Great idea, Harvey. The sooner the better."

Harvey then chimed in with, "As I sit here and think about this step—self-discipline—it sounds a lot like step number five: work conscientiously and productively."

Mr. Taylor said, "Step five is more about having a plan

and diligently pursuing it, whereas step seven is about being self-disciplined enough to master whatever it is you need in order to accomplish your objectives." Harvey was nodding even before Mr. Taylor finished explaining the difference.

DAILY STATEMENT
TO HELP ME MASTER STEP #7
SELF-DISCIPLINE

I am on the right track and am putting forth the time, energy and effort to learn and develop what I need to in order to become the person I'm capable of becoming and accomplish life's most important objectives.

STEP 8—BE A SELF-STARTER

"Harvey, SUCCESS IS NOT THE RESULT OF SPONTANEOUS COMBUSTION. ONCE YOU HAVE A PLAN, THEN YOU MUST SET YOURSELF AFIRE. You must be a self-starter. Only the amateur waits to be started by someone else.

"It follows, then, that you compete with your ultimate self. You are either YOUR worst enemy or YOUR best friend. You decide! The amateur competes with other people, and the pro always competes with her or his own ultimate self. If you overcome others, you may be STRONG, but when you overcome YOURSELF, you become MIGHTY. There are not many words that are more talked about and/or implied in business and in athletics than the word 'motivation.' Leaders sometime wear themselves out trying to get people to do what they want them to do. Self-starters are self-motivated. They don't need someone else to light their fire—they light their own fire and know how to keep it lit. They read inspirational books, listen to inspirational speakers on CDs, tapes, television or radio, and they stay focused on priorities.

Harvey responded, "I sometimes seem to get so bogged down in all the things I have to do every day that I feel absolutely overwhelmed. I wake up some mornings wanting to just hide under the covers because I'm already dreading what I have to do before I ever get out of bed." Harvey continued, "On days like that, I don't even want to think about motivation much less hear someone say, 'You can do it, Harvey—just suck it up and do it—go, Harvey—you da man." He chuckled as he lowered his voice with those last words.

Mr. Taylor laughed with him, "Harvey, listen to yourself. The more of those clichés and silly sayings you came up with, the lighter your mood became until you finally let out a laugh when you said, "You da man."

Mr. Taylor decided it was time to pick up the intensity. "Harvey, someone once said that the most important words we will ever utter are those things we say to ourselves, about ourselves, when we are off by ourselves. More people engage in negative self-talk than in positive self-talk. All those statements—like *I can't, I'm not smart enough* and *Who do I think I am*—literally become our self-fulfilling prophecy. Winners are constantly talking to themselves like everyone else. The BIG difference is they are saying things like, *I'm good at this. I'm smart enough, talented enough and committed enough to make this happen. Because of all that, it is going to be a great day.*"

Harvey seemed to sit a little taller as Mr. Taylor looked him right square in the eye and said, "Keep repeating positive self-talk, Harvey, and you will be amazed at how quickly your life will turn around. Write down everything you can think of to say to yourself and about yourself. Here, this will help," he said as he handed Harvey the worksheet for #8.

DAILY STATEMENT
TO HELP ME MASTER STEP #8
BE A SELF-STARTER

I will honor my possibilities by truly being a self-starter. I will not wait on anyone else to "start" me. I START myself. My positive self-talk will help me be a self-starter. I will start by writing out all the positive things I need to say to myself about myself.

STEP 9—OBEY THE LAWS OF MAN

"Before we continue to the next step, Harvey, let's refer back to our foundation—ATTITUDES. I just want to remind you how terribly important they are. Based on all we've talked about so far, wouldn't you agree that ATTITUDE is our FRAME OF MIND, and if the heart of a person is the engine that keeps him or her running, then the mind is the conductor? How do we know if the conductor is on the job? The only indicator of an alert conductor is to determine if the mind is thinking. Thought, then, is the mind at work, right? In other words, if a mind isn't thinking, it is dormant. Now, since all great ideas have come from the mind of man, thought must be the most productive form of labor. Doesn't that reinforce how important our thoughts are?"

Mr. Taylor continued, "Steps nine, ten and eleven take us to the three sets of Universal Laws. Understanding these principles will enable you to climb our visualized staircase more easily and with greater zest. The three are: man-made ordinances and statutes; physical laws; and the most powerful set, the spiritual laws. I only want to mention them briefly.

"Step number nine again is, 'Obey the Laws of Man.' If you violate a man-made law, such as exceeding a speed limit, and are caught, you'll be fined and possibly even imprisoned. It is simple. If we all strive to obey the laws we have created, we have a better chance of living in harmony with each other. If we ignore them, we can count on anarchy, chaos and an every-person-for-themselves world to live in."

DAILY STATEMENT
TO HELP ME MASTER STEP #9
OBEY THE LAWS OF MAN

I abide by and live, work and play within the laws of the land. I realize that traffic, civil and all other laws exist for a reason. I realize that laws and rules establish boundaries for an orderly way of life. Without law and order, we would have lawlessness and chaos.

STEP 10—OBEY THE LAWS OF NATURE

"OK Harvey, long before the laws of man were created, the laws of nature did and still do reign above them. If you violate a physical law, such as the law of gravity, and jump out of a tenth-story window, as someone once so aptly said, 'I guarantee you will not go northeast.' We also know that water is going to run downhill unless you pump it uphill, and for every action there is an equal and opposite reaction. Newton got bonked on the head by an apple because he was in the way of gravity's pull. Magicians, daredevils, circus performers and cinematographers try to make us think they have defied the laws of nature, but trust me: everything they do really is an illusion. It is not the way it appears to be. They will all tell you they have to use the laws of nature to make you think they went against them.

"The laws of nature are irrefutable. We don't question them. For instance we know that:

THE SHEEP THIEF

> What goes up must come down; at 32° Fahrenheit, water will freeze; heat water to 110° Fahrenheit, and it will turn into steam.

"There are two kinds of risks we can take, Harvey—physical risks and emotional risks. Both cause us to step into the unknown and/or maybe even sometimes into perceived dangerous situations. Without at least the perception of danger or failure, then it's not a risk. There are very few emotional risks from which we cannot recover, but there is a long list of physical risks that could permanently injure us or endanger us in some way. I'm not saying you shouldn't fly, climb canyon walls, ride motorcycles, or go scuba or sky diving if you are so inclined. Just know the risk and obey the laws of nature.

"In the laws of man, if you choose to drive twenty miles over the speed limit and don't get caught, you'll get to where you are going a little earlier than you would had you driven the speed limit. However, we know that if we get a speeding ticket, we'll have to pay a fine and maybe even have to endure traffic court—plus—if we are stopped, we'll end up getting to our destination a lot later than we would had we driven the speed limit. So the consequences of speeding involve time and money. However, when we defy or disobey the laws of nature, the consequences could involve pain, serious injury or even death."

Harvey sat quietly thinking about a friend he'd had in high school who chose to drive recklessly, rounded a curve one evening in a rainstorm, slammed into a tree and has spent the rest of his life in a wheelchair, unable to speak. He teared up as he thought about how his buddy had defied not only the laws of man but also the laws of nature, and how that combination had taken him to the brink of death.

DAILY STATEMENT
TO HELP ME MASTER STEP #10
OBEY THE LAWS OF NATURE

I will not let my need for excitement overrule my good judgment. I will be careful and take the necessary precautions in any activity, whether it is bungee jumping, sky diving, parasailing, ice skating, golfing, bowling, fishing or any activity in which I decide to participate.

STEP 11—OBEY THE LAWS OF GOD

"If you either willfully or unknowingly challenge one or more spiritual laws, you are flying in the face of universal forces that will defeat you every time. The great spiritual laws are all in the Bible. Even the works of other religions include the admonitions, concepts and laws that are in the book we know as the Bible. One of the books in the Bible known as one of the four gospels that begin the New Testament include the Beatitudes, given by Jesus to the multitudes in His Sermon on the Mount that I referred to earlier. You can find them all in Matthew, chapters 5–7. The end of Matthew, chapter 7, tells how the crowd responded to Jesus and why they responded the way they did. Jesus walked His talk and since He is God, He obeyed the laws of God.

"It's that simple. Live the way Jesus lived and you can't help but obey the laws of God. Keep reading the Bible and you'll find beautiful promises like 'Knock and it shall be opened unto you,' 'Seek and ye shall find,' 'Ask and it will be given unto you' and 'By their fruits ye shall know them.' The most powerful is the summary of truth called the Lord's Prayer. Study these truths, Harvey. Test them. USE them. They WORK!! They are the roots that nourish healthy and stretching attitudes. And, as we agreed, attitude is everything!

"And a vital part of the real renewal of your life is to know that you CANNOT really break any of these laws. YOU CAN ONLY BREAK YOURSELF UPON THEM if you do not seek to understand and apply them.

DAILY STATEMENT
TO HELP ME MASTER STEP #11
OBEY THE LAWS OF GOD

I will seek to better understand the laws of God by reading scripture every day, knowing that He showed us how to live, how to treat each other, how to treat ourselves, what to be concerned about and the rewards of a Godly life.

STEP 12—DEVELOP A DEEP PERSONAL RELATIONSHIP WITH GOD

"You must believe in God and develop a deep personal relationship with Him, Harvey. You must believe in something BIGGER than you before you can truly believe IN you. How can anyone look at this wonderful universe and not throw themselves down at the feet of a mighty God? The Hubble spacecraft sent back pictures of stars being developed and coming out of a colossal mass of dust and gas that is 7,000 light years away. Everything around us is so intricate in miraculous detail. As someone once said, to think our world and everything in it, on it and around it just came together is exactly like thinking that somehow a crystal from New Zealand, hands from Manitoba and little numbers 1 through 12 from a dozen different places somehow all came together to form a watch totally on their own without help from anyone. How much more complex is a tree or a bird or a human being? Isn't it even strange to think that everything just somehow happened all by themselves?

"God is the Great Creator. He alone made all that exists. The depth of our appreciation for the wonders around us is greater when we know the one who made it. That is why a relationship with God through Jesus Christ is so much more important than religion. God loves you, Harvey, and really does want you to know Him, to love Him and to depend on Him for all things. The best news I can give you, Harvey, is that if your relationship with God either doesn't exist or isn't where you think it ought to be, all you have to do is when you take this next step, include a request that He take complete control of your life and that His Holy Spirit enters your heart and makes you into a new person in Him. I promise you, He will hear you and He will answer your prayer."

DAILY STATEMENT
TO HELP ME MASTER STEP #12
DEVELOP A DEEP PERSONAL RELATIONSHIP WITH GOD

I believe that God is the creator of all that was, is and will ever be. I know He loves me and is at work in my life. I have a loving relationship with God and spend time with Him every day. He is Lord of my life.

Note: If you do not have a personal relationship with God and want one, it is the easiest, biggest and most rewarding step you will ever take. You can't work hard enough to earn it or be good enough to deserve it. All you have to do is what it says in the Bible. Acts 16:31: "They [Paul and Silas talking to the jailer] replied, 'Believe on the Lord Jesus and you will be saved.'" Pray this prayer right now. "Dear God, I do believe Jesus died for my sins. I accept Him as Lord and Savior of my life and want to spend eternity with you. Amen." If you'd like someone to pray with you or you want more information, call the author at 1-800-255-1982 or email him: al@alwalker.com.

STEP 13—PRAY

"Harvey, it might seem that what I'm about to tell you should have been included in the last step. However, I've made it step number 13 because it deserves special attention. There are four main thoughts I want you to remember about prayer.

"The first is that prayer for many people seems futile because they seek to TELL God what they want. They treat God like Santa Claus instead of like the loving Father that he is. They see him as someone or something they talk TO…not with. Prayer is conversation with God, and conversation is always a two-way street that involves both talking and listening.

"Second, when you have a conversation with a friend you talk about life—the good, the bad and all the in-between. God wants to hear all that. He wants to know what you're excited about, what is making you feel good or bad; He wants to hear about what you might think are the mundane things of life. He wants to laugh with you and cry with you. You are the most important thing in the world to Him."

"But God already knows all that, doesn't He?"

"Yes, He is omniscient, but He wants to hear it from you."

"The third thing is that God wants you to be specific. Somebody once said, 'When prayers are specific, results are terrific.' God does want the details, and He wants you to be clear about what you want. He wants you to name names, tell Him exactly what you'd like to have or see happen.

"Finally, one of the hardest things for most people to believe is that God ALWAYS answers prayer. What makes it hard is that either they weren't listening or God didn't provide the answer they wanted. Sometimes his answer is—'wait.' Believe me, Harvey, God's answer will not always be the exact answer you want, when you want it, but He will answer. Your prayer needs to include praise to God, thankfulness for all He's done for you, confession of sins, intercession (prayers for others) and attention to your own needs. Note, however, that Holy Scripture clearly says to ASK. And when we ASK with love and devotion and belief, we RECEIVE—again, not always what we want, but we do receive.

"The Bible says, 'The fervent prayers of a righteous man availeth much.' In other words, get right with God and then pray with all you have in you, and you'll get an answer—guaranteed. Here's the biggest part of prayer, and I mentioned it earlier—LISTEN. When you pray, Harvey, don't be in such a rush that you don't take time to listen to God. Will you actually hear God's voice? Maybe! Most will tell you that they've never heard an audible voice of God saying anything to them but what they have heard and what you will hear is that inner voice that tells you what is right, gives you guidance, tells you what to do and makes whatever situation you are dealing with a little clearer. You might not hear that voice the minute you pray, so keep praying; you will. I'm amazed at how people can continually have these one-sided conversations with God, then complain when they never get an answer. Prayer is like so many things, Harvey: the more we pray, the more comfortable we are with praying."

DAILY STATEMENT
TO HELP ME MASTER STEP #13
PRAY

I will spend time in prayer every day. I will keep a prayer list so that I can pray for the specific needs of others.

My prayers will praise God, express thankfulness for all God has done for me, seek forgiveness for my sins as I confess them, include my concerns for others and finally pray for myself. I know God already knows my innermost thoughts, yet I know He wants me to express those thoughts as I spend time with Him. I will remember to listen for that still, small voice. I will know when God is speaking to me.

STEP 14—GIVE

"Another vital ingredient in the joyful life, and part of the key to life's great treasure, is the importance of GIVING. This is the 14th great step. Calvin Coolidge put it well when he said, 'No person was ever honored for what he received. Honor has been the reward for what he gave.' An old Hindu proverb says, 'Help thy brother's boat across and lo! Thine own has reached the shore.'

"Money could never buy the warm impulses of the human heart, invariably producing greater happiness for the giver than for the recipient. You need something bigger than yourself to live for in order to have a successful and fulfilled life. The way in which you commit yourself to this rare and beautiful privilege of living will determine completely what you do with it. All too often we live at the level of the CRAFT of living and never even get a whiff of the ART of living.

"Abraham Maslow created a model in which he illustrated what he referred to as the hierarchy of needs. It says that self-actualization is the ultimate motivator. I believe that those who give a little even when they don't have much for themselves know the sweet taste of 'self-actualization' throughout their lives. A lady named Oseola McCarty gave Southern Mississippi University $150,000 when she was 89 years old. What made that so special was that she made her living washing and ironing clothes for other people. She charged 10 cents to do a bundle of clothes…10 CENTS, Harvey, and she was able to save enough money to give $150,000 to a school she had never attended. In 2001, *Worth* magazine named her as one of the top 100 people who changed the way Americans thought about giving. I'd say she was fully self-actualized, wouldn't you, Harvey?"

"I sure would. When I hear about people giving those size gifts, it sometimes make me feel like...well...if I can't give a lot, I just won't give any. I know that's not right, but what little bit I manage to scrape up to give seems so insignificant, even though I know every little bit helps. When I hear about someone like Oseola McCarty, it reminds me that even a little bit can help and can eventually, as she proved, add up to be a lot. I haven't been much of a contributor. I know I need to be more consistent in my giving. A few coins in the Salvation Army bucket at Christmastime assuages my guilt a little, but it certainly doesn't make me feel like a major contributor to the needs of our society. I want to take this giving step, so I promise to make it a part of my life."

"Here's the worksheet for 'Giving.' You need to think this through, Harvey. Who do you want to give to, how much do you want to give and when will you start? Like anything else, giving needs to be a part of your overall personal plan."

Mr. Taylor came to a stop. "We've made a lot of headway today, Harvey. Shall we call a halt to our proceedings?"

"Sure," said Harvey. "My head's swimming a bit right now. I've got some real work to do before we get back together. I need to go back and retrace a few of those steps before I'll be ready to move on."

Picking up several sheets of paper from his desk, Mr. Taylor handed them to Harvey as he continued, "Here are some thoughts to add to your notes and think about until next time. Remember, call me at 2577 when you're ready to get together again."

Harvey glanced at the neatly printed papers Mr. Taylor offered him. He smiled as he saw they were the distilled essence of everything they had been discussing. He looked over at Mr. Taylor, held his hand out and said, "I'll be looking forward to our next meeting," as Mr. Taylor left his office.

Harvey glanced at his watch. It was 2:15 p.m. The five hours they had talked seemed like five minutes. Surprisingly, they'd even talked right through lunch. Harvey laughed out loud as he thought, "I don't remember the last time I missed a meal, and I could stand to miss a few. Hmmm...looks like maybe some good changes are already happening."

DAILY STATEMENT
TO HELP ME MASTER STEP #14
GIVE

I have a lifestyle of GIVING. I give, not anticipating receiving anything, including recognition or reward. I give simply for the joy of giving.

CHAPTER VII
THE STEPS GET STEEPER

On Sunday morning, Harvey got up at 5:30 and spent a couple of hours reading back over his notes and the papers Mr. Taylor had given him. He also got his Bible out and studied Matthew 5–7. He found himself spending 30 minutes a day reviewing Mr. Taylor's steps of action. A little over two weeks later, on a Tuesday morning, Harvey was ready to pick up his phone and dial 2577. Mr. Taylor's melodious voice answered his call immediately, "Hello, Harvey."

Harvey, quite taken by surprise, asked, "How did you know it was me?"

Mr. Taylor chuckled, "I have my own version of caller ID—some call it intuition. Something just told me you'd be calling about now. Lucky guess…I guess."

Pleased that his call was evidently expected, Harvey said, "How about another get-together Saturday morning, and this time I'll come to your office?"

Mr. Taylor said, "No. Trust me, we'll be more comfortable in your office, Harvey. See you at 9:00 on Saturday morning."

When Harvey and Mr. Taylor met again, it seemed there had been no interruption at all. They seated themselves comfortably and Mr. Taylor resumed, "We're almost halfway with everything I shared with Jean and now with you, Harvey. At this point, we should be ready to do some serious climbing up that imaginary staircase. The rest of the way can be fun and exciting even though it's tough. Are you ready?"

Harvey smiled. He was ready! He felt he had truly started to absorb what Mr. Taylor had talked about and was ready to learn more about the climb. The planning sheets with the affirmations on them had been a great help. He found himself repeating them throughout the day. He'd even taken the time to write each affirmation on a 3x5 card. Carrying the cards with him seemed to help.

STEP 15—BE A PERSON OF INTEGRITY

"OK, here we go! This next step, Step #15, permeates everything we are discussing in these sessions, Harvey. Integrity is applied honesty. It is what you ARE, not what you SAY. Ann Morrow Lindbergh said, 'The most exhausting thing in life is insincerity.' Insincerity is dishonesty, and honesty is the bedrock of integrity. Without integrity the next step is not possible, because integrity and strength are synonymous. Integrity is measured by what you do when no one is looking.

"Congruency is the secret to integrity. What I mean by that is that if your actions are not congruent with what you say, then you are not a person of integrity. The common term is 'sending a mixed message.' Here's an example.

"One evening a father came home to find his son using several different colored markers as he drew a picture. The father did not recognize the markers, so he asked his son where he'd gotten the markers. The son said he'd brought them from school. The father then said, 'Son, you know you can't bring things from school. Those belong to the school, and for you to bring them home is stealing. Next time, just let me know what colors you need and I'll bring some from the office.'

"Sir Francis Bacon said, 'It's not what we eat but what we digest that makes us strong; not what we gain but what we save that makes us rich; not what we read but what we remember that makes us learned; and not what we profess but what we practice that gives us integrity.'"

DAILY STATEMENT
TO HELP ME MASTER STEP #15
BE A PERSON OF INTEGRITY

I am a person with the highest levels of integrity. I AM who I SAY I am. Who I am thunders so loud that I don't have to tell anyone I'm a person of integrity.

STEP 16—RESPECT YOURSELF

"This leads us to Step #16—respect for YOURSELF. The sum of your strengths and your integrity comprise your feelings about yourself. If these feelings are right and you can truly ACCEPT yourself, then you can focus your energy on others and on what you are doing instead of yourself. It all begins with YOU. We can change our whole life and the attitude of people around us simply by changing OURSELVES. When I came to truly understand that, Harvey, the change in my life was enormous. When we learn to respect ourselves, we find other people more enjoyable and easier to get along with. Close on the heels of respecting yourself is BE YOURSELF—and do it with humility. How many arrogant, obnoxious blowhards do you know, Harvey? We've all been around at least one or two in our lifetime, haven't we? Yet, how many genuinely authentic people do you know, Harvey?"

"Jean Bennett," Harvey thought. "If there's ever been anyone to whom the saying '*what you see is what you get*' applies, it's Jean. No pretentiousness at all."

Mr. Taylor didn't wait for an answer other than the nod he got from Harvey, and he went on, "The blowhards are always bragging on themselves, telling us how great they are, the many grand and glorious feats they've accomplished and how much better they are at anything than anyone else could ever hope to be, and the loudest among them is the most insecure. Authentic people, however, with high levels of self-respect can focus all their attention on others. Your actions always speak so much louder than your words. Don't tell me how wonderful you are. Show me. When we respect ourselves and like who we are, even though we are conscientiously striving to continue to be all God intended us to be, we are content. People who are insecure measure their success against others they see as being successful and confident. Allowing others to be the determining factor in your self-esteem is ludicrous. The best measurement of success is when we measure ourselves against...ourselves."

DAILY STATEMENT
TO HELP ME MASTER STEP #16
RESPECT YOURSELF

I respect myself, and that enables me to respect others. I see the more perfect attributes in myself and others, and I do not focus on the imperfections. I strive daily toward even greater authenticity.

STEP 17—LOVE

"Here's Step #17: We can learn respect for ourselves and other people more easily when we understand the power of love. Love is the most powerful success vitamin in the world, and it is also the toughest, most difficult, yet most effective emotion of us human beings. You're looking puzzled, Harvey. Do you have a question?"

"Could you elaborate on love a little bit more? I know we use the word 'love' to mean everything from 'I kind of like' to 'I can't live without' and dozens of other degrees of both. We tend to say, 'I love this cookie I'm eating,' and then turn to someone we care deeply about and use those same words. I know love is powerful, but with the multitude of ways we use the word, don't we weaken it and rob it of its power?"

"Yes, I agree completely with you, Harvey. We do overuse and misuse that word, yet it is still a very powerful word. Love is magnificent medicine for the ills of the whole human race, because to really love is to care about others as much as, or possibly even more than, ourselves, and to want the good which life offers them, both for them and for ourselves. If you truly believe this and can communicate it through your words and actions, you can dissolve virtually any problem that may arise in your life."

Mr. Taylor sat up in his chair and leaned toward Harvey when he said, "Here's the real power in the word. It's self-love—not narcissism, but a genuine love for your uniqueness, for all you are and for all you are capable of becoming. Sure, there are things about yourself you need to work on, like lose weight or maybe improve your physical condition. All of us need to work on ourselves, but in the meantime, we should love who we are, no matter what the shell is like. To me, bringing that word full circle means you must love yourself as well as others. Matthew 19:19b says, '...and love your neighbor as yourself.' Another way to rephrase that might be—'There's no way you can love your neighbor the way you ought to if you don't love yourself the way you ought to.' If you don't see anything in yourself to love, you won't be able to truly love anyone else. Love says to others 'I want to know and understand you better.' But it all starts with loving yourself. Someone once said, 'If you don't love yourself, that probably makes it unanimous.'

"What is the opposite of love, Harvey?"

"Hate?"

"Yes, and it is also a powerful word. Yet where love can bring joy and energy, hate brings fatigue and pain. The most destructive emotion is hate. The brilliant educator Booker T. Washington, the first teacher and head of Tuskegee

University from 1881 until his death in 1915, faced prejudice all his life, but he made a very significant choice about how he would handle it: 'I will never allow another man to control or ruin my life by making me hate him.' One big burst of negative anger is more fatiguing than an average day of work. Hate and pain are inseparable. It requires some time and possibly trial and error to fully understand what love can do, but it really works. So much of what we've talked about and will talk about later includes love.

"I also believe in tough-minded love, Harvey. Sometimes as a leader or a parent, we have to do some tough things we'd rather not have to do, like give a bad financial report to a board of directors or discipline an employee or a child. Yet all of those are made a little easier if we have genuine love in our heart. I've known people who were so worried about being seen as a pushover and as being weak that they came across harshly when it wasn't necessary. If you really want respect in this world, respect others enough to deal with them from a position of love. That's the power I mentioned earlier."

DAILY STATEMENT
TO HELP ME MASTER STEP #17
LOVE

I will exemplify tough-minded love in all I say, do and am. I believe love truly is invincible.

STEP 18—THINK EDUCATION

"Education is not a destination, but a continuing journey, so always believe you can learn more. Rigid thinking is to take dead aim on rigor mortis, the ultimate state of rigidity. An open mind can grow and never stop growing. A closed mind dies.

"One of the reasons mature people stop learning is that they become less and less willing to risk failure by going beyond the FAMILIAR. I have had the opportunity to meet and know some beautiful people who were still living abundantly in their 80s and 90s.

"Robert LeTourneau, an incredibly successful entrepreneur, was known as 'God's Businessman' because he dedicated 90 percent of his company stock to the LeTourneau Foundation, which sponsored Christian missions in South America and Africa and financed LeTourneau Technical Institute from its founding in 1946 until 1961. He also was a pioneer in establishing an industrial chaplaincy for his employees, and he traveled each weekend to speak to large audiences about applying Christian principles in everyday life up until his death at over 80 years of age.

"Lillian Gilbreth, who lived to be 92 and was known as the 'Mother of Modern Management,' is another example. She and Robert LeTourneau had widely varying degrees of formal education, but they had the same attitudes toward personal growth and development. Norman Vincent Peale was a vigorous and dynamic person up until his death at the age of 95. They each helped prove that long, happy, abundant lives are products of being very concerned about, and open to, the needs and richness and uniqueness of other people and other ideas. They all continuously pushed themselves to read and learn and grow.

"Dr. Peale attributed his longevity to two things—his faith in God and his high level of curiosity.

"Harvey, curiosity can certainly apply to formal education. However, a curious mind seeks knowledge everywhere. What do you need to know that you don't know? Do you want to know more about social networking or how to be a better fly fisherman or how to be a culinary genius in your own kitchen or how to write a strategic plan for your business? Whatever it is, the resources are at your fingertips.

Read, study, learn, grow and read some more, study some more."

Harvey interrupted, "I get it, I get it. You are right. I need to decide what I need to know that I don't know or need to know better and go after it."

DAILY STATEMENT
TO HELP ME MASTER STEP #18
THINK EDUCATION

I believe wisdom is the result of both formal and informal education plus experience. I have a high level of curiosity. I push myself to gain new knowledge and develop new skills.

STEP 19—THINK QUALITY

"Step #19 is 'Think Quality' in everything you do—quality in ideas, in human understanding and in every facet of your life. When you place quality first, quantity comes in abundance. A quality INNER life leads to the rich and abundant TOTAL life, makes you what you are, and what you are makes others want to hear what you say. We usually think in terms of product or service quality. How do we determine quality, Harvey?"

"Does it meet certain standards…is it up to par, up to snuff, up to speed, things like that," Harvey replied.

Mr. Taylor half frowned, half smiled and raised his eyebrows at the clichés: "OK, what do those mean?"

Harvey chimed in with, "They mean that something is at the level it needs to be."

Mr. Taylor nodded. "Let's take another tack—what do you mean when you say someone is a quality person?

"I mean they are a good person, a person who shows good character traits, a person with high standards."

"Exactly," Mr. Taylor exclaimed. "Great character and high standards—seems to me then that there is a better chance that an individual like that will more than likely provide products and services that are high in quality."

"That makes sense," Harvey muttered as he nodded his head.

"Which step is this, Harvey?"

Harvey looked back at his notes and said, "Number 19."

"Correct. Now, do you see how the steps depend on each other? You can't have a quality person who isn't clear about the very first step. If our values aren't nailed down, it's much easier to justify diminished quality in our lives and in whatever we do, and as it says in step two—whatever we say. When we face difficulties, if we haven't come to grips with step four—being willing to attempt the difficult, we'll have a tendency to settle for less. Harvey, if you've truly understood and absorbed the first 18 steps, step number 19 is a whole lot easier."

DAILY STATEMENT
TO HELP ME MASTER STEP #19
THINK QUALITY

Everything I do reflects my appreciation and respect for quality. I take the time to do the job right the first time. I am proud of every job I do because I put my best self into each one.

STEP 20—LISTEN POSITIVELY

"If you want to take the life, warmth and spontaneity out of a relationship, Harvey, just start listening inattentively. Look away while they are talking. Better yet, start talking to someone else while the first person is still talking and always reply before the other person is through talking.

Constantly interrupt; always try to top their story; be totally insensitive to their reactions to what you are saying; never ask any questions and never LOOK like you are listening."

As Harvey and Mr. Taylor laughed at the sarcasm, Harvey said, "I can give you names of a couple of people who are just like that right here at Millspring." Mr. Taylor smiled and said, "So listen positively. Listen with your guard DOWN and concentrate, in order to truly let the other person into your heart. Harvey, I've heard all my life that the opposite of talking, for most people, isn't listening—it is waiting—waiting for their turn to talk. Instead of concentrating on what the other person is saying, they are thinking about what they are going to say at the first opportunity, and the split second the other person takes a breath, they jump in and start talking.

"The negative listener hears the other person out and then SAYS WHAT THEY WERE GOING TO SAY ANYWAY.

"Conversation requires the ability to ask meaningful, interesting questions and to listen with all pores open. In his classic book, *How to Win Friends & Influence People*, Dale Carnegie tells the story of being at a dinner party and sitting on the edge of his chair talking with a world-famous botanist the entire evening. At midnight, he said his goodbyes and the host later told Mr. Carnegie that the botanist had commented to him that Mr. Carnegie was "most stimulating" and a "most interesting conversationalist." Mr. Carnegie later commented that he had hardly said anything, primarily because he didn't know anymore about botany than he did the anatomy of a penguin. He said he listened because he was intently interested and kept asking questions, which encouraged the botanist to talk. He went on to say, 'That kind of listening is one of the highest compliments we can pay to anyone.'

"What is the most basic objective of any conversation? To

understand and to be understood! Effective communication is shared meaning and shared understanding. When the communicatee doesn't understand exactly what the communicator intended, some of the blame can be attributed to both parties. Maybe the communicator assumed too much or didn't use the right words and the other person was confused, distracted or didn't understand and didn't want to ask. There is usually enough blame for everyone involved. Let's get beyond blame and look at one of the major reasons some people are 'listening challenged.'

"Because our brain can process information faster than someone can speak, it is easy to take a mental side trip while someone is talking. When we do, we often miss something they said and don't realize it. Have you ever been around someone who drones on and on about something and never seems to be able to get to the point?"

"That's when I catch myself taking those side trips you mentioned," Harvey said. I sometimes even realize I've been daydreaming for I don't know how long. I just want to shout, 'Come on; hurry up; spit it out.'"

Mr. Taylor smiled his all-knowing smile and said, "In the middle of that daydreaming and inattention is where we miss important information. It is a challenge, and those people who have learned to concentrate on what someone is saying seem to have fewer misunderstandings."

Harvey laughed and said, "That reminds me of a comment a friend of mine made not long ago. We were talking about this very subject of people not listening, and he said, 'I think of myself as a pretty good listener but the other day my wife said I never listen to her, or something like that,' and we both laughed."

Mr. Taylor chuckled and said, "Even good listeners need to concentrate and work on their listening skills and especially when those closest to us are talking. The main thing I want you to take away from this, Harvey, is the importance of concentrating 100 percent on what someone else is thinking.

"Ready to take the next step?"

Without saying anything, Harvey nodded and turned the page in his binder and waited on Mr. Taylor's next words of wisdom.

DAILY STATEMENT
TO HELP ME MASTER STEP #20
LISTEN POSITIVELY

I am a very good listener. I focus all my energy on the person talking. I clear my mind and concentrate on what is being said. I look the person in the eye, and my facial expression tells them I'm listening.

STEP 21—EXPECT THE BEST

"We all have problems in our lives. How we deal with them and our attitude toward them, Harvey, make the difference between a stagnant, unhappy life and a joyful life. A troubled person once asked the great preacher, speaker and author Norman Vincent Peale how he could rid himself of all problems. Dr. Peale said, 'I can direct you to a place where there are 1,500 people who have no problems whatsoever.' When the man answered, 'That's the place I want to go.' Dr. Peale directed him to a nearby cemetery. To have problems, to identify them and to welcome them is NOT only to have proof that you are living, but it is an EXCELLENT WAY TO HELP ENSURE that you will live longer and better. Problems are really opportunities and possibilities in disguise. Someone once said that those who do not have problems to solve are out of the game. Be grateful for problems, Harvey.

"Walter Brennan said, 'If you help the chick out of its

shell while it's hatching, it's going to be too weak to survive. It's the STRUGGLE that develops its muscles.' That's #21, Harvey. Welcome problems and see them as an opportunity to grow and develop. Someone was overheard to say, 'When I don't have problems, I wonder why God doesn't trust me anymore.' We hear and read a great deal today about tension and stress. Negative, frightened, self-centered and internalized tensions can make you ill. But positive, strength-oriented, goal-centered, problem-solving tension can help ensure health, youth and joy. Positive stress says you are ALIVE and CREATIVE and WELL. It is the electric current your personal motor must have for real results.

"I don't know of any sport that doesn't start with 'get ready.' Most plays in football start with 'Ready...set…" Tennis, golf, you name it—you have to get set—get ready before you do anything.

"Why?" Mr. Taylor asked rhetorically. "To muster all your strengths, focus on the job at hand, get yourself aligned and send the right signals from your brain to your body and its muscles. It's what I call 'alert expectancy.' Something is about to happen and I want to be ready and alert. I also want to have an attitude of positive expectancy. People often handicap themselves from the start when they go into any situation expecting bad things to happen. If you concentrate on the bad stuff, then bad stuff is what you're probably going to get. Focus on what you want to happen next. If an athlete keeps saying, "I'll never make that shot," more than likely he won't. Even though saying, 'I'm going to make this shot' doesn't guarantee success, it sure gives you better odds of making it because you are sending the right signals to your body.

"There are five basic steps to problem solving, Harvey. First, we have to ask, 'What is the problem?' Charles Kettering, an engineer and the inventor of the electric starter, said, 'A problem well stated is a problem half solved.' The second step is to identify all the causes of the problem, and we need to keep digging until we find the real cause—the root cause. The third step is to explore all possible solutions and look at every possible option. Step four is to decide what the best solution is, and the final step is to take action.

"Here's my last thought on problem solving, Harvey. If after you have looked at a problem from every angle and there is absolutely no solution in sight (even though there is usually always something that can be done), put it behind you and move on with a clear head asking, 'OK, what is the next problem? Sitting around stewing over something for which there is absolutely no resolution is a complete waste of energy and time. Worry is not a solution."

DAILY STATEMENT
TO HELP ME MASTER STEP #21
EXPECT THE BEST

I am a problem solver who expects a positive solution. I look for the best in everything and everybody, knowing that I must focus on the best outcomes in life and not the worst. I am known as a person of action.

STEP 22—SPEAK UP

"Now we come to learning to think and speak crisply, decisively and confidently. When you radiate assuredness in your speech, Harvey, you provide reassurance to all around you. Whether your conversation is one on one, within a small group or to an audience of thousands, the ability to confidently and coherently express yourself is powerful. Who would you want to follow, someone who is timid and unsure of themselves or someone who is bold, able to make decisions and knows how to speak in a way that is inspiring, uplifting and encouraging?"

Mr. Taylor had hit a nerve in Harvey, and both of them knew it. Harvey could talk to anybody one on one, but he hated having to speak in front of any group—no matter what the size—from two on up. He always felt like he was being put on the spot and didn't like the spotlight being put on him. He also knew several people in the company who always seemed so relaxed and confident whenever they spoke…whether it was prepared or spontaneous. Jean Bennett was one of those people.

Mr. Taylor didn't want to stop there and let Harvey wallow in his negativity so he asked, "Harvey, I know you're OK one on one. What is it that bothers you about speaking to more than one?"

Harvey thought, *He's reading my mind*, and said, "I don't know, I just seem to stumble; say things I wish I hadn't said; look back on things I should have said and didn't. It's like, if I have to stand to talk, my mind sits down and abandons me."

Mr. Taylor chuckled and then realized Harvey wasn't laughing, so he said, "Harvey, the great speech trainer and coach I mentioned earlier, Dale Carnegie himself, once said, 'There are always three speeches for every one you actually give. The one you wanted to give, the one you gave and the one you wish you'd given.'

"I know some people seem to be more at ease with speaking and that the majority of people would rather die than have to speak, yet I've never known anyone who, if they were willing to work at it, couldn't master the art of speaking. And by the way, as far as I know, no one has ever died from speaking."

As Harvey laughed, Mr. Taylor went on. "Ask anybody to list the top ten speeches ever recorded in the history of man and you'll get all sorts of answers. Which ones come to your mind?"

"Lincoln's *Gettysburg Address*, Martin Luther King's *I Have a Dream*, and…Winston Churchill's *Never Quit* come to mind the quickest," Harvey shot back.

"Those are usually on most people's list," Mr. Taylor told him. "Others include Patrick Henry's *Give Me Liberty or Give Me Death*, and several will mention Ronald Reagan's *Tear Down This Wall* speech. Most of us will not have the opportunity to make a speech that will be heard around the world, but we do know that all great leaders have the ability to confidently express themselves. Benjamin Disraeli said, 'Talk to people about themselves and they will listen for hours.' Someone else once said, 'The best way to sound like you know what you're talking about is to know what you're talking about.'

"Remember, Harvey, your physical posture, presence and bearing speak eloquently to all who see you, even before you utter a sound. You show your attitude toward life by the way you communicate. Help in speaking is available to anyone who wants it…but the best way I know of to get better at speaking is to speak—as often as you can. Harvey, you know that the best way to overcome any fear is to do that which we fear the most. OK, that's Step #22. Your willingness to put some effort into this tells us whether you CONFRONT and ENGAGE life, or take the expedient way out. Choosing the expedient and easy path each day is a sure invitation to mediocrity, disappointment and despair, and leaves your physical, mental and spiritual muscles weakened."

Mr. Taylor then shifted gears, took a deep breath and said, "After we talk about this next step, Harvey, I think we'll call it a day for this session, if that is all right with you."

DAILY STATEMENT
TO HELP ME MASTER STEP #22
SPEAK UP

I know that leadership gravitates to those people who can effectively express themselves. I am actively seeking opportunities to speak. I spend time preparing my thoughts. I practice what I plan to say, and I speak with confidence.

STEP 23—LIVE POSITIVELY

Harvey nodded and Mr. Taylor continued, "Live, talk and work positively. This means you are consistently and constantly looking for the light. You are reaching OUT. You are unwilling to waste time exploring the darkness where only the lonely and discouraged dwell. Remember, Step #1 was what?"

Harvey didn't hesitate and quickly said, "You become what you value."

"Exactly," said Mr. Taylor, "and the second step was..." And Harvey chimed in with, "You become what you SAY." Mr. Taylor then said, "Applied thought is the most productive form of labor. The fused and focused power of the human mind can dwarf the mightiest atomic bomb in sheer strength. The human brain possesses more computative units than the most sophisticated computer in the world. A dozen Pentium Plus microchips are only tools waiting for a human brain to make them usable. Even Big Blue, the once heralded megacomputer from IBM, needed human beings to make it a chess champion.

"Live, talk and work in terms of what you are FOR. Waste no time simply thinking about, dwelling on and working in terms of what you are AGAINST. Step #23 is LIVE POSITIVELY.

"How much easier, more helpful and effective it would

be if people would state what they are FOR and not just what they are against. For example, don't just tell me you are against sin, but FOR virtue; that you are just against crooked politics, but FOR sound government; that you are just against illicit sex, but FOR sound, sanctified married love. A person who is always AGAINST is turned inward. Yet one who is FOR is moving FORWARD and takes a much stronger position. Tell me what you're for, Harvey. If we agree, I'll follow you almost anywhere. But, if all I ever hear is what you're against, I'll begin to see you as a negative person and will begin to avoid you completely.

"Ready to call it a day?" Mr. Taylor asked. It was now a little after 1 p.m. and Harvey could tell Mr. Taylor was a little tired. What Harvey didn't know was that Mr. Taylor had decided to start acting a little tired in order to give Harvey an out and allow him time to go home and think about everything they had discussed.

He was positive Harvey couldn't absorb much more.

"Sure," Harvey replied, "until next time."

They both got out of their chairs, and as Mr. Taylor turned to go, Harvey said, "I think I'm going to stay here and clean up my notes a little while they are still fresh on my mind." They shook hands, and Mr. Taylor left Harvey to his thoughts.

Around 4:30, Harvey realized he'd stayed a lot longer than he'd planned on staying, plus he had not even stopped for lunch and his growling stomach told him he needed a bite of something. Harvey walked to his car deep in thought about all he and Mr. Taylor had discussed.

DAILY STATEMENT
TO HELP ME MASTER STEP #23
LIVE POSITIVELY

I make a conscious decision every day to live with a positive attitude. I am open to all sorts of possibilities each day will bring. I live each day seeking to have a positive influence on everyone and everything.

CHAPTER VIII
FINISHING THE CLIMB

STEP 24—CARE

The following week, Harvey called that now-familiar 2577 extension and set another time to get together the next Saturday. Once again, Harvey offered to come to Mr. Taylor's office, but again, Mr. Taylor insisted on coming to Harvey's. As they sat down Saturday morning promptly at 9 a.m., Harvey told Mr. Taylor how things were at work. He told him that in the month since the announcement that he definitely had not wanted to hear, he'd seemed to be more on track than he'd been in a while. He told Mr. Taylor about how the president of the company, Doc Henry, had even been by to see him and commented about how well he'd handled everything, that Doc knew he'd been disappointed in not getting the job as director of operations, but Doc had been getting feedback that Harvey was not letting that get in the way of his work. Mr. Henry told Harvey he was proud of the work he was doing and even told him he was someone they were counting on for the future.

Mr. Taylor smiled, and told Harvey he was not one bit surprised. Then he picked up as if they had only taken a short break.

"This next step, Harvey, is about a word I'm very fond of. That word is CARE. If you CARE enough you can find out who you really ARE! If you also learn to give enough and care enough not only about your own goals and dreams but about the goals and dreams of others and how everything and everyone fits into a grand design that is much, much bigger than any of us, you will come to know who you really are and what your ultimate place is in that Grand

Plan called LIFE. You have all the opportunity you could ask for to target total fullness as a person; as a unique and real YOU. Zig Ziglar said, 'You can have everything in life you want, if you will just help other people get what they want.'

"Men like Lee Iacocca, Fred Smith, Ross Perot, John Teets, Rich DeVoss and Bill Gates did not invent or create primarily to get rich. Their PRIME MOTIVATION WAS TO CREATE A BETTER WORLD!! They knew they were on to something that would make a significant difference in the world. Because they were committed to this, because they cared very much about what they were doing and they cared about others, their fellow men made them rich. You will be able, if you CARE enough, and I bet you do, to prove that continuous renewal as a total person can be yours. BUT you must visualize yourself as a walking transmitter of enthusiasm, energy, gusto and integrity on the job and off. Radiate joy and the truth is, joy will find you.

"Show me someone who only talks about themselves, only thinks about themselves and is out to get what they can at any expense, and I'll show you someone who never learned the lesson that when you care about the welfare of others, they'll care about and appreciate you more than you can ever imagine."

Mr. Taylor's comments made Harvey think about a poem or a statement he'd run across some time ago and remembered he'd saved it in a Word document he'd titled as "Quotes" that he used to save stuff like that when he ran across it. And while Mr. Taylor was talking, Harvey grabbed his mouse and clicked on Word, went straight to his documents and scrolled to the one titled "Quotes." As soon as he opened it he scrolled down and there it was—a piece that had been found on the wall of Mother Teresa's home for children in Calcutta.

He printed a copy and realized Mr. Taylor had stopped

talking. When it came out of his printer he handed it to Mr. Taylor and said, "Doesn't this kind of sum up what you've just been saying?"

Mr. Taylor started reading the piece of paper Harvey had handed him, and a smile came across his face because, yes, he had seen this piece several years earlier. He also fondly remembered one of the greatest caregivers he'd ever known, Mother Teresa. "Harvey, this is the version on the wall of the Shishu Bhavan, the children's home in Calcutta, India, that was written by Mother Teresa. Her version is pretty close to the original, but she only included eight of the original ten 'paradoxes.' The original was written by Dr. Kent M. Keith when he was a 19-year-old student at Harvard as part of a student handbook for student leaders entitled *The Silent Revolution: Dynamic Leadership in the Student Council*, published by Harvard Student Agencies in 1968, and he titled it *The Paradoxical Commandments*. You're probably not going to believe this, but I carry a copy of it with me in my pocket." And Mr. Taylor reached into his coat pocket and pulled out a laminated pocket card containing Dr. Keith's original *The Paradoxical Commandments* and handed it to Harvey as he said, "Keep it, I have more copies in my office."

The Paradoxical Commandments
by Dr. Kent M. Keith

1. People are illogical, unreasonable, and self-centered. Love them anyway.
2. If you do good, people will accuse you of selfish ulterior motives. Do good anyway.
3. If you are successful, you win false friends and true enemies. Succeed anyway.
4. The good you do today will be forgotten tomorrow. Do good anyway.

5. Honesty and frankness make you vulnerable. Be honest and frank anyway.
6. The biggest men and women with the biggest ideas can be shot down by the smallest men and women with the smallest minds. Think big anyway.
7. People favor underdogs but follow only top dogs. Fight for a few underdogs anyway.
8. What you spend years building may be destroyed overnight. Build anyway.
9. People really need help but may attack you if you do help them. Help people anyway.
10. Give the world the best you have and you'll get kicked in the teeth. Give the world the best you have anyway.

As Harvey sat there reading the commandments, he just shook his head in amazement at how often Mr. Taylor seemed to have just the right thing or thought or idea or whatever was needed at any given moment. He was very intuitive, insightful, ingenious and the wisest man Harvey had ever known or just old, lucky and knew a few things... Harvey chuckled at how ridiculous those last thoughts had been. He knew he was sitting with one of the most brilliant, well educated, articulate, thoughtful and genuine human beings on the planet, and he was indeed privileged to have Mr. Taylor take an interest in him.

"Harvey, I have a suggestion to make. When we finish with this session, go to www.kentmkeith.com. That's where I go to order these cards. You can also learn more about Dr. Keith and his work."

Harvey wrote down the web address as Mr. Taylor continued.

DAILY STATEMENT
TO HELP ME MASTER STEP #24
CARE

I am passionate about life. I care about myself and others. My passion comes through in everything I do. My passion stokes not only my own internal fires but the fires of others and causes them to want to do whatever needs to be done. I care.

STEP 25—DREAM

"Harvey, a dream is that most precious part of us which is personal, unique and real. Our life can have a rich tempo and pace when it is fed by a dream. We either build or destroy with every thought, word and action! Since we can't live in neutral, there is no in-between! We must put MUSCLE into our dreams.

"Harvey, please memorize this poem and then frame it and hang it on a wall:

Isn't it strange
That Princes and Kings
And Clowns that caper
In sawdust rings,
And common people
Like you and me
Are builders for eternity?

Each is given a bag of tools,
A shapeless mass,
A book of rules;
And each must make
Ere life is flown

THE SHEEP THIEF

A stumbling block
Or a steppingstone

R. L. Sharpe

"Think about it, and think about it, and think about it some more.

"Harvey, speaking of thinking, you're going to think I'm nuts when I share this next thought...but hear me out. If you still don't have a dream you can think of or are pursuing, I want you to come up with a really bad dream right now."

Harvey raised his eyebrows, lowered his head and asked, "A bad dream?"

Mr. Taylor laughed and said, "Spell 'bad' for me, Harvey."

"B – A – D," Harvey snickered.

"Now write down those three letters vertically—one letter right below the other—an acronym. Out beside the letter B, write the word BIG; beside the letter A, write AUDACIOUS; and beside D, write DARING. Harvey, you need one huge, hairy, overpowering and powerful dream that challenges you, excites you, and inspires you to go after whatever that BAD dream is. You've heard the term *deal breaker*?" Harvey nodded. "Well, here's a life's deal MAKER—everyone needs a great BAD dream, and no matter how big you think you're dreaming—dream bigger.

"Someone once said, 'Go ahead and shoot for the moon because even if all you do is clear the treetops at least you will have proven to the world you can fly.'

"OK, Harvey, let's get real serious for a minute. This is the one area in which I've had the biggest challenge with people I've worked with in the past. There are three aspects of dreaming in order for a dream to really be a BAD dream.

"To begin with, most people have trouble busting out of their mental shells and emotional encrustation and allow ing themselves to dream of doing, having and accomplishing things that some might call laughable. As a matter of fact, if your friends and family don't laugh at your dream and call it crazy, your dream is not big enough. If you never hear comments like *Who do you think you are? Nobody in our family has ever done anything like that. You got your head in the clouds*, or any variation on those themes, you're guilty of either not dreaming big enough or not ever telling anyone about your dreams. What do you reckon the friends and family of the Wright brothers said when they told them they were going to build a flying machine? Wonder what Noah's wife told him when he said he had a dream that he should build a massive ship in the desert? Every great invention came from big dreamers.

"Do you think Mark Spitz who won seven gold medals at the Olympic Games in Munich in 1972, or even better, Michael Phelps who won eight at the Olympic Games in Beijing in 2008, thought of themselves as just run-of-the-mill swimmers who just enjoyed doing a few laps in a pool somewhere? Of course not. They dreamed of standing on that center platform with gold hanging around their necks, and then they went about doing whatever they had to do to make that happen.

"The second thing is a comment Dr. Greg Barr made once in a sermon. He said, 'If your dreams don't involve other people, they are too small,' and I agree with him.

"There are thousands of examples of people and organizations that dreamed huge, over-the-top, truly Big, Audacious and Daring dreams and accomplished what they dreamed and then some. The sad truth is that there are tens of thousands of very talented and gifted people on this planet who haven't had a dream, or if they did, they didn't believe in it enough to do what they had to do to make it a reality.

"As soon as they come up with a wonderful dream, they start telling themselves all the reasons they won't or can't accomplish it. They'll tell themselves they don't have the talent, skills, abilities, resources, stamina or whatever else they think they'll need to realize their dream. Harvey, I want you to hang on to this next question, which is the third aspect of a BAD dream.

"Would God give you the intelligence necessary to come up with a massive dream and then not give you what you needed to make it a reality?" Mr. Taylor sat quietly as that last question sank in.

"Great dreams generate great goals and great plans within which we can involve others, set timetables, objectives, bench marks, etc., all of which put muscle and energy into our dreams."

Harvey sat quietly thinking about how much he wanted to be a good father, have a good home, be a leader in the company, make an impact on and a difference in the world, do something significant. He could see all of those, but that one big BAD dream didn't seem to materialize for him right now—yet he did feel different. He felt like maybe the fog was lifting and that he was beginning to see what he was supposed to be doing, who he was supposed to be and where he was supposed to be heading. When he looked up, Mr. Taylor was smiling and he said, "It'll come… It'll come… Let's move on."

DAILY STATEMENT
TO HELP ME MASTER STEP #25
DREAM

I believe in the power of a huge dream. I know that no matter how big I dream, I can dream bigger. I dream big dreams that I turn into objectives, goals and timetables with accountability.

STEP 26—STAY HEALTHY

"Step #26 involves your health." Then Mr. Taylor asked, "When was your last physical?"

Harvey said, "It's been a while—but," he quickly added, "after writing out my values back in step one, I called and have an appointment for a full physical in about six weeks."

Then Mr. Taylor said, "Wonderful. In addition to getting checked out, I want to encourage you to press your doctor to tell you how fit you can possibly become through EXCELLENCE in diet, exercise and wholesome living habits. If your doctor is not inclined or qualified to do so, GO TO A DIFFERENT DOCTOR. Then set out to discover how it feels to REALLY FEEL GOOD. I mean JUST AS GOOD AS YOU POSSIBLY CAN!! Probably one in ten thousand people at most truly feel AS GOOD AS THEY CAN. Believe it or not, it requires courage to properly handle a body that is just as fit and joyful as it can be. One of the areas in which I asked you to write your values back in step one was Health. What did you write about that area?"

Harvey flipped back in his notebook to his values statement that was about seven pages long, found what he'd written about health and said, "I consciously think about my physical health and condition on a daily basis. I drink lots of water, take vitamins, eat the right foods and exercise at least three times a week for an hour or longer. I schedule a thirty-minute quiet time every day for reading and reflection, plus I have regular check-ups with my doctor."

Harvey looked up as Mr. Taylor asked, "How's that working for you?"

"Well, I really just got started. I am drinking more water, and I joined a health club and so far have had two sessions with a personal trainer who really seems to know what he's doing. He pushes me, but has started me off kind of slow and easy because he said he wants me fit,1 not sore."

"I'm proud of you, Harvey. Physical and mental health play such an important role in our lives, and I'm glad to see you seized the opportunity to get started. A word of warning, though—don't get frustrated if you don't see immediate results. The fact that you've seized the moment, started doing something and are committed to being consistent is the key to improved health. Goethe said, 'The right man is the one who seizes the moment.' WHILE WE MEDITATE ON WHEN TO BEGIN, IT BECOMES TOO LATE TO DO SO!

"Robert Louis Stevenson died at the age of 32, but he probably did more real quality living, loving, giving and building during those 32 years than most people do in a longer lifetime. And it was Stevenson who said, 'That man is a success who has lived well, laughed often, and loved much; who has gained the respect of intelligent men and the love of children, who has filled his niche and accomplished his task; who leaves the world better than he found it, whether by an improved poppy, a perfect poem or a rescued soul; who never lacked appreciation of earth's beauty or failed to express it; who looked for the best in others and gave the best he had.'

"I've often wondered how many more great words of wisdom he could have passed along had he lived longer."

DAILY STATEMENT
TO HELP ME MASTER STEP #26
STAY HEALTHY

I am committed to feeling as good as I possibly can! I have a physical and mental health plan, and I exercise both of them regularly.

STEP 27—PRACTICE AGAPE LOVE/SERVICE

Mr. Taylor paused again, his voice became softer, and he began to speak in an almost reverent tone.

"We're very close to the top of the stairs now, Harvey, and I would like to quote the One who said it even better than Stevenson, and who was also the architect of modern phrases like 'management by results' and 'management by example.' HE said in the Sermon on the Mount, 'By their fruits ye shall know them.' HE also said, 'You are the earth's salt' and 'You are the world's light,' and 'The Kingdom of God is within you.' He also said, 'I am the vine and you are the branches. If any man abides in me [which means *stays connected to me*] and I in him, he will bear much fruit. But apart from me, he can do nothing.'

"Harvey, I know that 'balance' means different things for almost everybody. I don't know what a 'balanced' life looks like for you. I do know that we need to figure that out for ourselves and at least be conscious of the amount of effort and resources we put into work, love, play and worship. One of those four words is one we discussed earlier—love. Remember, we discussed earlier how tough and strong and stretching that four-letter word is. We both know that love has a broader meaning than the erotic love of man for woman. It also includes filial love, which is a feeling of brotherhood, a warm sharing of cooperation, concern and openness. Step #27 is a third dimension of love, and the TOUGHEST, of this powerful word. It is AGAPE LOVE, the strong and selfless emotion in which you care more about another person or persons than you do about yourself. It is different than the caring we talked about in step #24; agape love is self-giving, self-sacrificing love that knows no boundary. When you use the word 'love,' Harvey, it's important to know which definition you're using.

"Christopher Morley said, 'If we discovered that we had

only five minutes left to say all we wanted to say, every telephone would be busy with people calling other people to stammer that they love them.' Don't wait until the last five minutes. Do it TODAY!

"Have you ever belonged to a service club or a community service group?"

"Does the Chamber of Commerce count?" Harvey asked.

"Sure does...along with civic clubs and other community organizations. What's important, though, is that you're actually doing something if you belong to one of those and not just getting your name on a list so you can use it as a resume builder. Plus, there are a multitude of organizations through which you can show agape love...your church or synagogue; a professional organization or association; neighborhood associations and especially some of the family aid groups like soup kitchens, food pantries, meals-on-wheels, and many more.

"To be a person who loves the whole of mankind is to be intimate with life's innermost secret. You are also carrying out and demonstrating the truth of Gandhi's great statement about finding yourself by losing yourself. Gandhi said, 'You will find yourself by losing yourself in service to others, your country and your God.'"

DAILY STATEMENT
TO HELP ME MASTER STEP #27
PRACTICE AGAPE LOVE/SERVICE

I believe in Agape Love. To love others in a total self-giving, sacrificial way—to do whatever it takes to meet the needs of others. I am excited, even intoxicated, by the insights and possibilities inherent in the truth, "By their fruits ye shall know them."

STEP 28—HELP OTHERS FIND THEIR WAY

"A few final thoughts for you, Harvey. Here's step #28. Look back in your notes and tell me what step #3 was." Harvey flipped back through his notes to step #3. "Build on strengths."

Mr. Taylor went on, "We've talked a lot about caring and about agape love. A fine way of expressing both of those is to help others discover, surface and realize their strengths.

"A few years back, Jim Collins wrote a book called *Good to Great*, in which he talked about not only getting the right people in an organization, which he referred to as getting the right person on the bus, but that we had to make sure they were in the right seat on the bus. One of the most valuable leadership skills is the ability to not only identify people's strengths but then also being able to help them see those strengths in themselves and then utilize them effectively. The big question in this step then is, 'How do you successfully identify strengths in other people?'"

Harvey chimed in, "Observation? You watch them, work with them, spend time with them, and their strengths will eventually surface?"

"What about someone you've just brought on your team, or even better, someone you're interviewing for a job?" Mr. Taylor asked.

"Look at their resume, their track record, work experience, etc.," Harvey answered.

"Does that really tell you their strengths?" Mr. Taylor asked.

"No, I guess not. It just tells me what they've done."

"Exactly."

"Why not just ask them what their strengths are?" Harvey shot back.

"Remember what a challenge it was for you when you began writing a list of your strengths?" Without giving

Harvey a chance to reply, he went on, "Then how hard do you think it would be to really discern someone's strengths just by asking them what they are in an interview?"

As Harvey thought, Mr. Taylor continued, "Here's a way to help them do that. Instead of just asking them to list their strengths, ask them to describe for you the greatest success they've had in their life. As they tell you their story, look for strengths they demonstrated or utilized to achieve that success. When the story is over, tell them the strength(s) you identified. Who knows? You might even identify a strength they weren't aware of.

"Patrick O'Brien, in his landmark book *Making College Count: A Real World Look at How to Succeed in & after College*, describes how he used that method when he interviewed college seniors for jobs with Procter & Gamble. He said that P&G wanted to hire leaders, but if you simply asked a group of college seniors if they were leaders, they would all say yes. He knew that wasn't always the case, so he would ask how many of them had been involved in at least two organizations on campus. Those that didn't raise their hands, he let go. Then he'd ask those who remained for a show of hands of those who had served as an officer in that organization. He'd weed the group out even more with that question. Then he'd interview the remaining people individually and ask them to describe a project they initiated that made a difference in their organization. He was able then to identify leaders because he knew he could discover if they really had demonstrated leadership characteristics through their stories.

"We can do the same thing with anybody, Harvey. Just ask them about their successes, their wins, their accomplishments, and then LISTEN for strengths. More important, tell them what strengths they used and, who knows, you just might help someone discover something about themselves that they either didn't know or were unsure about. As a result, they may then capitalize on that newfound strength to do more in their career and life than they would have had you not helped them see that which was already there.

"Harvey, these next two steps are really important even though I'm not going to dwell on them. You need to make sure you understand them clearly."

Harvey nodded as Mr. Taylor went on.

DAILY STATEMENT
TO HELP ME MASTER STEP #28
HELP OTHERS FIND THEIR WAY

I look for the strengths in others, and I tell them how their strengths are helping them. I believe in building people up, not tearing them down, in strengthening them and in helping them discover their gifts, talents and abilities.

STEP 29—HIGH EXPECTATIONS OF OTHERS

"Harvey, one of the ways we can help others overcome bland ambitions and end up settling for far less than they are capable of achieving is to raise our expectations of and confidence in them. The best way to help someone grow is to challenge them to do something they don't think they can do."

Mr. Taylor smiled as he remembered what he was about to share with Harvey.

"Several years ago I was coaching a young man in our human resources department to be a better instructor for one of our programs. He had watched some of our senior instructors on several occasions, taken pages and pages of notes, practiced on his own, and the day came for him to help teach a class in one of our branch offices. I'd told him we would teach the class together. We agreed to meet at a restaurant at 6:30 a.m. to go over our notes and make any last-minute preparations before we went to the office around 8 a.m. The class was scheduled to start at 8:45 a.m. The branch office is about three hours away, so we'd made reservations at a hotel close to the office for the night before.

"What he didn't know was that I had to cancel my reservation at the last minute but had decided not to tell him. The next morning around 6a.m., I called him on his cell phone and told him something had come up where the president of the company needed me in another situation and that I would not be there to help him teach the class that morning, but that I knew he could handle it on his own.

"You should have heard him. He started with things like, 'But I've never taught this class. What if I blow it? What if I forget something? What if I…,' and I stopped him and said, 'You've studied, you've taken tons of notes, you've practiced and I KNOW you are ready…plus they won't know what you don't tell them. I know you'll do a great job and I can't wait to talk to you when the class is over and hear how it went.'

"I've heard him tell that story of how I abandoned him in his moment of greatest need and then he'd laugh and add, 'But it was one of the best experiences of my life. I grew more that day than I ever realized I could.'

"Harvey, I could have been there that day, but I knew he was ready and the best way to prove that to him was to simply throw him into the deep end of the pool where he had to swim or drown. I knew he was ready to swim.

"By the way Harvey, if you ever want to talk with him about what happened that day, go see Lou Petty, our vice president of human resources."

Harvey was surprised to hear that Lou had ever been fearful of teaching because he was known not only throughout their company, but he was also known as one of the best speakers and teachers in their industry. He'd heard Lou on several occasions and thought about how much he wished he had the ability to stand in front of a crowd of people and hold them in the palm of his hand like Lou could.

Harvey thought Mr. Taylor must have been reading his mind when he said, "Harvey, I've seen you in some of our company meetings, and when you spoke about things for which you had a real passion, you really had an impact on the group. You could be as good as Lou if you put some effort into it.

"Step #29 is to have high expectations of others. Once people realize you have more confidence in them than they have in themselves, they will work hard to prove you right. Expectives are stronger than directives. They get better results! Directive living leaves off where expective living starts."

DAILY STATEMENT
TO HELP ME MASTER STEP #29
HIGH EXPECTATIONS OF OTHERS

I have high expectations of others. Along with challenging myself, I challenge others by giving them opportunities to do things they didn't think they could do, encouraging them along the way and cheering for them as they succeed.

STEP 30—LEAD BY EXAMPLE

"One of my favorite Latin phrases, Harvey, is 'Exemplum Docet' which means, 'The Example Teaches.' Step #30 is to know that the great leaders of history not only had high expectations of themselves and others but they also led by example and asked much from their followers.

"How many times have you heard the saying, 'I'd rather see a sermon than hear one'?"

"Oh, I don't know…a couple of hundred?" as they both laughed.

"Harvey, if you want to be a great leader, you've got to study, understand and apply the characteristics, skills and abilities of great leaders. You don't have to reinvent the wheel, but you sure do need to study the wheel—take it apart and put it back together. You need to learn by example before you can lead by example. When you were a child, did your parents ever say something like, 'You need to set a good example for your younger brother or sister' or for some other younger child in your family, church or neighborhood?"

"All the time," Harvey said as he continued, "I have a younger brother, and my parents stayed on my case about setting a good example for him."

"Harvey, being a great parent, leader, citizen, spouse, sibling, boss, manager or leader requires us to be aware of the example we're setting for others. Here's another way to look at it. What difference would it make in this world if everyone really strived to be the kind of person they thought others thought they were or at least hoped others thought they were? What if we all consciously tried to be the parent our children really thought we were and lived the example of a mature, confident, compassionate and loving mom or dad? What if we modeled what a really good parent looked like? Wouldn't our children have a better chance of becoming better parents themselves?

"There's hardly a grandparent on the planet who hasn't overheard one of their children talking to their own children in a less than positive way and realized they were hearing themselves in their child's voice and regretted it, wishing they could go back in time and set a better example."

Mr. Taylor could tell this was all sinking in when Harvey echoed, "Be the person I want others to think I am. That's kind of like the saying, 'Feelings follow action.'"

Mr. Taylor smiled, "Exactly, and a great thought. How many times have people made some statement like 'I'll do so and so when I feel like it' because they didn't understand that concept—that feelings follow action. Harvey, you know there are days when you've not felt like being a leader, but you led anyway; days that you didn't feel like being a parent, but you did what you needed to do anyway; days when you didn't feel like cutting your grass or paying your bills or working on some project, but you did anyway and once you did, you felt the feelings that had kept you from doing it in the first place. Great leaders get that and are aware of the example they are setting for others—every day."

"Whew!" Harvey exclaimed. "That's like throwing down my own gauntlet at my own feet to challenge myself to be the person others think I am and lead by the example they need me to be. Talk about upping the ante."

The smile had not left Mr. Taylor's face, and he knew Harvey was ready for the final step.

DAILY STATEMENT
TO HELP ME MASTER STEP #30
LEAD BY EXAMPLE

I believe that the best way for me to demonstrate my leadership abilities is by my example. I will constantly study and seek to emulate the example of the One who said, "Follow me."

CHAPTER IX
BEYOND THE DOOR

"Now, Harvey, we approach the SUMMUM BONUM, another Latin phrase, meaning, 'the highest good,' 'the distilled essence' or 'the one great secret,' of a renewed life. It provides the mortar for cementing together the great principles of: BUILDING ON STRENGTHS and recognizing that YOU BECOME WHAT YOU THINK and that YOU BECOME WHAT YOU SAY and all the other concepts we've been discussing.

"This is the final step on our mythical stairway. You have reached the door. In just a minute, we're going to open the door to the ultimate statement of truth. It's staggering in its sheer practicality. It's just on the other side of the door. But first, as you look back over the 30 Steps, put a check mark by the ones you need to work on the most. How many did you check?"

Harvey replied quietly, "All of them, but seven of them really stand out that I need to work on."

Mr. Taylor then said, "Close your eyes and imagine us standing on Step #30. The door in front of you has 30 deadbolt locks on it. They are numbered one through thirty. Put your key in each of the seven locks you need to work on and turn it. When you turn the key in the final lock and hear the deadbolt snap back in place, push the door open, open your eyes and read out loud the words in front of you. When you open your eyes, Harvey, you'll see the final and greatest of all instructions ever given to man. They'll be the first thing you'll see when you open the door."

With his eyes closed, Harvey mentally put the key in each lock and turned it. He saw himself open the door. He opened his eyes, and right in front of him the tall, white-haired, well-dressed Mr. Taylor was holding a single 3 x 5 card on which was written:

Step 31

Love the Lord your God with all your heart and all your soul, and all your mind; and your neighbor as yourself.

Because he could tell this was not what Harvey had expected, Mr. Taylor said, "Examine and test this power-packed answer from every angle, Harvey. Do it thoughtfully, respectfully, openly and curiously. If you do, I promise you an unusual life with unusual growth and unusual joy.

"As your mind and spirit grow and reach upward and outward, so that the things you THINK and SAY and DO and ARE are the things that the great Commandment of LOVE unleashes, let yourself savor the perpetual SENSE OF WONDER about everything around you.

"Then, you will know, as your friend Jean Bennett found, the joys of a wonder-FULL job, wonder-FULL human relationships and a wonder-FULL life."

Harvey leaned up in his chair, put both elbows on his desk and his head in his upturned hands and just stared at the card as Mr. Taylor put it down in front of him. They both just sat quietly with neither saying a word for several minutes.

Mr. Taylor finally smiled understandingly. "What we have been talking about, Harvey, is a LIFELONG JOURNEY." As he spoke, he handed Harvey a folder. "These are all statements of tested truth. You can build them into your very being by tackling these repeatedly one at a time. Especially the seven you said needed the most attention. This can be your blueprint, the action plan we discussed earlier. You have a lot of work to do, but it will be a labor of love. Keep this 3 x 5 card handy until you memorize it.

THE SHEEP THIEF

"You've been a wonderful student, Harvey, and even though we won't be having any more meetings, I'm sure I'll be kept informed about your progress. I wish you the very best. And, Harvey, I want to give you something to remember our time together."

Harvey laughed and said, "I promise you there is no danger of my ever forgetting our time together."

Then, Mr. Taylor reached in his coat pocket and handed Harvey a small three-inch-square package and said, "Wait 'til I'm gone. Then open it."

They stood and shook hands, and as Harvey watched his new-found mentor leave his office, he knew his life would never be the same again.

As Harvey opened the small package, he saw a pair of the most beautiful, 18-carat gold, oval cuff links he'd ever seen. Engraved in the center of each cuff link in very majestic old English script were the letters ST. Along with the cuff links was a card. Harvey's eyes watered as he read the simple message:

> Dear Harvey,
>
> These letters don't have to be branded on your head for the world to know you're a saint. Just live like one every day. And wear these as a reminder of two things. The first is of our time together, and the second is that you are becoming a saint on earth when you follow the path we've been discussing. Remember, always be the sheep thief who DIDN'T run away no matter how difficult things may seem.
>
> Love,
> Seth Taylor

As he thought back over the sessions he'd had with Mr. Taylor, he decided to call and thank him for this extraordinary gift. He dialed extension 2577 and got a sterile recorded message that said the extension was not assigned to anyone. He'd called it so many times, he assumed he'd just misdialed; so he punched out 2 - 5 - 7 - 7 again and got the same recording.

He called the operator and asked her to dial it. They both heard the same recording. He then asked her to dial Seth Taylor's office for him. She came back a second later and said, "We don't have anyone by that name who works here."

"Sure we do," Harvey said. "I've been meeting with him here in my office."

She simply said, "I'm sorry. There's no one by that name on my register."

Harvey hung up the phone and went to the elevator, which he took to the 25th floor. As he got off, he stepped up to Margaret, who had been running the executive floor for years. She was as much a fixture at Millspring as...well, she was Millspring and, most important, she knew everybody. After they had exchanged pleasantries, Harvey said to her, "I'd like to speak with Mr. Taylor."

Margaret said, "Nobody by that name up here. What department is he in?"

Harvey said, "I don't know. I thought he was up here. He told me he was on Millspring's board of directors."

Margaret said, "Nope. You might check with personnel, but I know I've never heard that name, and especially not as it relates to our board. What is his first name?"

"Seth," Harvey told her. "Mr. Seth Taylor."

Harvey felt totally confused and went back to his office and called Jean to tell her what had happened. They both spent time trying to find Mr. Taylor.

And, for the next few days, every time Harvey put on the cuff links with the letters ST, he thought of the greatest mentor he'd ever known. There were times when he was thinking about Mr. Taylor that he remembered seeing an image of some sort on the old man's forehead. It had appeared to be just aged skin. Then, the more he thought about it, he began to realize the vague image on his head was two letters—letters that before had not really been noticeable. But now, in his mind, Harvey could see Mr. Taylor sitting in front of him with the faint outline of the letters ST becoming clearer and clearer on that dear face. Harvey said to himself, "I gotta be seeing things. My mind is playing tricks on me." He picked up the phone and called Jean. Harvey asked Jean if she remembered seeing anything on Mr. Taylor's forehead. The line went totally silent. After what seemed an eternity, Harvey said, "Jean, are you still there?" and Jean said, "Yes, I'm still here."

Then she said, "Harvey, when I'd finish my sessions with Mr. Taylor, it seemed that all I could think of was the story about the sheep thief, and I began to imagine having seen that ST brand on Mr. Taylor's forehead myself. But I didn't say anything mainly because there was no one to tell. When I told you about him, I wasn't sure enough to say anything even then."

Jean went on, "When I left your office that Friday afternoon after I'd just been promoted and bumped into Mr. Taylor in the garage, what I didn't tell you was that I knew he wasn't in our garage when I walked out to my car. However, as I punched the button to unlock my door, when I looked up, he was standing there—right beside my door and he quietly said, "Hello, Jean"—and it was like seeing God Himself. We hugged and as we pulled back from each other, but still very close, he said in his soft but strong kind of way, 'How's Harvey doing?' It really caught me off guard, and I wondered if he knew I'd just been with you."

Jean continued, "I told him a little bit about our conversation and that you would be calling him Monday. He congratulated me on my promotion and told me how proud he was of me. We hugged again, and I told him how much he meant to me. Then we shook hands and said good-bye. I then got in my car, turned the key and when I looked in my rearview mirror, there he stood—right behind my car. After I looked down to put my car in reverse, I glanced back and he wasn't there. I put the car back in park and jumped out thinking maybe he'd fallen, but Harvey, he was gone. I mean he was absolutely nowhere to be seen. I looked around the garage but couldn't find a trace. As I drove home, I couldn't help but wonder things like, "Why hadn't I seen Mr. Taylor walk up to my car?" and "People don't just disappear like that—particularly older people." He must have just hurried off while I was getting the car started, and I convinced myself that I'd wanted to see him so badly and had been so overjoyed by our brief visit that I just imagined seeing him behind my car. I forgot about the whole thing until today. And now I clearly remember as I pulled away from hugging Mr. Taylor that day in the garage, even though the letters were barely visible because of his age, I know I saw the letters ST on his forehead."

Over time, Harvey and Jean became closer than brother and sister. They helped each other along the way and today Jean is president, and Harvey eventually got his big promotion and is in charge of all operations at Millspring Industries. They are both setting the example of true leadership and what it means to genuinely enjoy what you are doing for all of the people who work with them.

Meanwhile, across town in another office building, a young lady who felt like her world was coming to an end sat staring out her office window. Suddenly, she was distracted from her self-absorption by a gentle knock on the wall just inside her door. She turned to see a very distinguished, white-haired gentleman wearing a blue suit and a big warm smile. She didn't notice the cuff links at first, but she did hear him say, “Hello, my name is Seth Taylor. I’m a special advisor to the board of directors here at Alco. Do you have a minute?”

CHAPTER X
SUMMARY OF STEPS

1. You become what you value.
2. You become what you say.
3. Build on STRENGTHS.
4. Attempt the difficult.
5. Work conscientiously and productively.
6. Laugh often.
7. Be self-disciplined.
8. Be a self-starter.
9. Obey the laws of man.
10. Obey the laws of nature.
11. Obey the laws of God.
12. Develop a deep, personal relationship with God.
13. Pray.
14. Give.
15. Be a person of integrity.
16. Respect yourself.
17. Love.
18. Think education.
19. Think quality.
20. Listen positively.
21. Expect the best.
22. Speak up.
23. Live positively.
24. Care.
25. Dream.

26. Stay healthy.
27. Practice Agape love/service.
28. Help others find their way.
29. High expectation of others.
30. Lead by example.

31. THE SUMMUM BONUM

LOVE THE LORD YOUR GOD WITH ALL YOUR HEART AND ALL YOUR SOUL, AND ALL YOUR MIND; AND YOUR NEIGHBOR AS YOURSELF.

PART II
MR. TAYLOR'S LEADERSHIP TOOL KIT

CHAPTER XI
THE MEETING

Time went by, and Harvey focused with real intensity on the 31 Daily Statements. He knew he was changing and growing. Ellen, who became his wife a few months after his time with Mr. Taylor, was delighted with the new Harvey. His sense of wonder, his joy and his attitude were contagious. Ellen and the two daughters she had from a previous marriage and Harvey's three children asked for their own copies of the Daily Statements. Eventually they decided to hold monthly meetings around the dining room table and share experiences, setbacks and suggestions.

Harvey continued to meet with Jean from time to time, and, at the end of the first year, he said, "I'm feeling so great about the new me...my new confidence... I'd like to make a suggestion."

"Fire away," said Jean.

"OK, here goes. Let's develop a comprehensive blueprint for becoming a leader—in EVERY dimension of our life, including life here at Millspring. Based on the understanding we both have from our work with the elusive Mr. Taylor, we could develop practices that would strengthen anyone who applied them."

Jean agreed, and they scheduled a meeting for the following Saturday at 9:00 a.m. in Harvey's office.

Sitting down at the conference table on Saturday morning, Harvey noticed a nice-looking, leather, three-ring binder in the middle of the table. He picked it up. Embossed in gold on the front were these words: A LEADERSHIP TOOL KIT FOR SAINTS. He flipped open the cover, read the first page and immediately looked around for evidence of Mr. Taylor. He jumped up and darted out in the hall. Jean followed with, "Hey! What's wrong?"

Harvey didn't see or hear anyone. He walked back to the conference table and shoved the book toward Jean without saying a word. Jean opened the book and read the following note:

> Dear Harvey and Jean,
>
> I know both of you are doing extremely well. Congratulations on your promotions. How does it feel to be running the show?
>
> I've kept up with you probably a little better than you think I have, and I did get word about this meeting you're having this morning. I wanted to add my thoughts. So, I had a friend drop this off at your office. Read it and then give me a call at Ext. 2577 if you have any questions.
>
> With love and respect,
> Seth Taylor

Jean and Harvey lunged for the phone. Jean got to it first and hurriedly punched out the number 2577, and, sure enough, Seth Taylor's voice came through loud and clear. Jean immediately hit the speaker button so that Harvey could talk to their mentor also.

"Hello, Harvey. Hello, Jean," Mr. Taylor said. "I'm surprised you've had time to look through the book I sent over."

"We haven't looked at it," said Harvey. "Where are you? I came up to your office and they'd never heard of you and this phone line."

"I know, I know," Mr. Taylor said. "That's not important. What is important is that you can get me when you really need me. And to answer your question about where I am—I guess I'm like both of you, I'm where I need to be. Like I said in the note, read over the material and call me if you need me."

The line suddenly went dead, and they both went back to the conference table stunned and speechless. It had been so long since they had talked to their mentor. Jean then read the memo out loud that was under the handwritten note:

TO: Harvey Cole and Jean Bennett
FROM: Seth Taylor

These techniques will help you forge a superb team at work and at home. Work daily at mastering and applying every item. Read each one and answer the two questions that follow. Determine which idea you need to work on the most, then the second most important and so on until you have prioritized all 45 ideas. Once you two understand them, pass them on to your people. You're both excellent speakers. Maybe you could get people together and conduct training sessions where you share these ideas. You know where to find me if you need me.

CHAPTER XII
45 TEAM-BUILDING IDEAS

1. Delegate in terms of results expected. Reward for actual achievement rather than activity.
   How?
   Why?

2. Make sure you are doing the right thing before concentrating on doing the thing right. Involve your team members whenever feasible and hear them. Together you can identify the right thing.
   How?
   Why?

3. Make sure that team members understand precisely how much authority they have in order to accomplish agreed-upon standards and expected results. Base all assignments on the creative and logical deployment of strengths. Search constantly for new strengths in your team members.
   How?
   Why?

4. Let team members make their own decisions whenever feasible and practical. Self-led teams and self-led individuals functioning within a total organizational process are the way to get things done.
   How?
   Why?

5. When you're deciding to promote a person, do not be overly influenced by his or her technical skills, even

though we all know those are critical. Recognize that interpersonal or "people" skills are what really get results. Every productive breakthrough in history has been of, by, about and for PEOPLE. Nothing productive happens without people.
How?
Why?

6. Remember that a fine example is worth ten thousand words. One can only follow a person who lives, talks and works in terms of what they are for. It's impossible to follow a person who is simply against events, things, people and life.
How?
Why?

7. Make sure that deviations from agreed-upon expectations are dealt with when they happen. Also that superior performance is recognized immediately. Incessantly and continuously expect the best!
How?
Why?

8. Problems of attendance, punctuality and accidents should be dealt with immediately, not deferred. And remember, your values are what you use in deciding and acting on problems. Cultivate the right values—individually and organizationally!
How?
Why?

9. Control your negative emotions. Leaders who blow hot and cold keep people feeling insecure and relatively unproductive. Relish, however, the experiences of

constantly providing earned praise.
How?
Why?

10. Take care of the company, and it will take care of you. As we sow, so shall we reap. Good givers ultimately become rich in every way.
How?
Why?

11. Try to make sure your people would say of you, "I always know what is expected, and you take the time to explain why."
How?
Why?

12. Vary your reading, and look for opportunities for new experiences so that you are constantly becoming broader and more informed about other facets of your organization and the world around you. The future is truly exciting for the person who is constantly learning.
How?
Why?

13. Try to become known by your fellow leaders as an unusually cooperative and supportive person. Never forget that people will not consistently follow a knower. They will virtually always follow a learner.
How?
Why?

14. Strive to always think before you act, then be decisive, follow through, and expect commitment and results. Accountability is the clear understanding that one does

a job or gets out of it.
How?
Why?

15. Be a concerned leader rather than a worried one. "Worry" can induce indecision and procrastination. "Concern" stimulates positive action.
How?
Why?

16. Recognize that, with skill and effort, you can help increase your people's hope in every performance appraisal and in all kinds of face-to-face situations. Hope is the universal motivator. With plenty of hope virtually anything is possible.
How?
Why?

17. Never overlook a valid opportunity to reinforce or build people in the eyes of their peers. Real leaders love to empower, enhance and build others.
How?
Why?

18. Flexibility, Imagination, Resourcefulness and Enthusiasm add up to FIRE. Put some fire into yourself, your people and your job. Negativism, fear and resentment can turn the hottest fire into the cold ashes of futility.
How?
Why?

19. Believe and expect all team members to be creative or at least contribute to the process. Constantly treat them as walking bundles of possibilities and strengths.

Expect their best!
How?
Why?

20. Learn to listen with both your mind and heart. Really hear what people say. Try to identify and relate to the unique dignity and hidden strengths in all people. See and sense their fears, hopes and aspirations.
How?
Why?

21. Shun defensiveness. Defensive people and actions only shrink and go backward. Emotionally vulnerable people grow, cope and become strengthened. We decline and decay in direct proportion to the growth of our defensiveness.
How?
Why?

22. Make your schedule realistic. Develop deadlines only after you have carefully considered all the potential problems in the people, money, material, time and space available to you. Then proceed to focus unwaveringly on your people's identifiable and latent strengths.
How?
Why?

23. Gossip and innuendo have no place in a top-notch organization, department or family. Make sure your example and expectations reflect this. Real leaders know there is no substitute for warm, positive candor.
How?
Why?

24. Strive constantly to become a skillful questioner. Learn

to probe, analyze and examine before forming a conclusion. Consistently ask, listen and hear in order to determine the wants, needs and possibilities of the team or family member.
How?
Why?

25. Study report writing. Learn to present performance data with clarity, brevity and validity. Obsolete managers focus on "activity data," while tough-minded leaders focus on results and performance data.
How?
Why?

26. Organize yourself so that time becomes an asset, not a liability. For instance, make weekly and daily lists of your most important musts and wants, prioritize both lists and stick to your order of priority. Defer all wants until each must is done.
How?
Why?

27. Improve your speaking skills. Do such things as practice with a digital recorder. Maybe hire a speech coach to help you. Work on pace, relaxation and warmth. Be guided at all times by a commitment to honor your audience.
How?
Why?

28. Know the difference between delegation and abdication. Delegation means to assign, trust, instruct. If needed, provide for orderly and mutually agreed-upon feedback with the full realization that you are still accountable for seeing that team members understand

and fulfill their responsibility, authority and accountability. Abdication means to relinquish all control and follow-through, and just hope the assignment gets done somehow. Passive abdicators quickly get left behind. Passionate delegators lead us to tomorrow.
How?
Why?

29. Stay healthy and fit. There is nothing more practical than to have your body, mind and spirit functioning as well as circumstances permit. You are able to think better, make better decisions and lead better. People feel drawn to the leader who is physically, mentally and spiritually fit. In 1873, Edward Stanley said, "Those who think they have not time for bodily exercise will sooner or later have to find time for illness."
How?
Why?

30. Expect to succeed. Expect excellence from yourself and your colleagues. Clear and positive expectations (or motives) are the basis for all productive motivation. The alternatives are just not acceptable.
How?
Why?

31. Organize meetings this way:
    - Carefully prepare your agenda.
    - Encourage the ideas and critiques of all. Draw them out. Ask, listen and really hear.
    - Make sure all members know the objective of the meeting.
    - Request feedback to ensure understanding.
    - Conclude the meeting with a summation of the

accomplishments and course of action agreed upon.
- Thank the group members for their participation and cooperation. Honor your audience. Expect their best!

How?
Why?

32. Skill and firmness in asking will virtually always accomplish more than ordering. Telling, pushing and driving compress and repress others. Asking expands, stimulates and actualizes others.
    How?
    Why?

33. Condition all working relationships and decisions with the belief that people should not be evaluated on the basis of color, creed, sex, age or religion. Rather, they should always be evaluated in terms of accomplishments and performance. Emphasize inclusion not diversity.
    How?
    Why?

34. To cope with unsatisfactory team members:
    - Avoid hiring a potential problem. Screen very carefully.
    - Stay in close touch with your team so that potential problems can be discovered early and dealt with.
    - Make sure they know precisely what the job expectations are. This should always include what, when, who, how and why.
    - Make sure they have all the materials, tools and coaching they might need.
    - Make sure your example is what it should be.
    - Be candid, be specific, build on strengths, listen and hear.

- Assume the team member is right until proven wrong.
- Get to know team members as well as you can. Attempt to help them see and feel a relationship between the priorities, expectations and rewards.
- Do not terminate employment without having carried out the above steps and making very sure they have understood exactly what the situation is.

How?
Why?

35. Remember that discipline is defined as "training that builds and strengthens." When the leader applies this approach with diligence, integrity and warmth, the number of unsatisfactory team members decreases significantly. Discipline must always enhance rather than diminish the team member.
How?
Why?

36. It is rare to find a case of absenteeism if team members are well coached, are in the right job, know what is expected, and are empowered and truly led.
How?
Why?

37. The first hour of the first day on a new job exerts a profound influence on the team member. Make sure the team member:
    - Feels expected and accepted.
    - Is encouraged to ask questions and is given thoughtful and thorough answers.
    - Feels part of a careful, thought-out orientation procedure.
    - Is helped to thoroughly understand the new job.

- Ideally, learns of the uniqueness of the company and is helped to feel truly a part of it.

How?
Why?

38. Make sure the team is enlightened, empowered, energized and enthusiastic.
How?
Why?

39. Share your vision, share your values, share your vitality. Among other motivational benefits, this will enhance shared meaning and shared understanding.
How?
Why?

40. Make sure your example and expectations call for continuous change. Constantly practice constructive discontent.
How?
Why?

41. Stay perpetually unsatisfied with quality in every dimension of your life and your area of operation.
How?
Why?

42. You can only lead others where you yourself are willing to go.
How?
Why?

43. Cultivate the art of concentration, intensity and focus. The only difference between a room full of light and an

awesome laser beam is the difference in intensity and focus.
How?
Why?

44. Attitude is everything. You can if you think you can.
How?
Why?

45. Negative criticism of others is the hallmark of failure.
How?
Why?

CHAPTER XIII
SEVEN TIMELESS TRUTHS FOR THE LEADER OF THE FUTURE

1. A leader provides transcendent or macro vision and magnetic life and pull, like a compass. A leader provides purpose and direction.

2. A leader provides a crystal-clear focus of all strengths in the organization. Knowing our strengths is our tool. A tough-minded leader expects and reinforces the best.

3. A leader is committed to people, service, innovation and total quality. A leader believes this commitment is liberating and enriching for all.

4. A leader leads by example that is focused, stretching and positive. A true leader is motive led and value fed.

5. A leader ensures that all compensation is related to positive performance and expects total integrity. A true leader is guided in all decisions by these two components:

   The problem is not the "competitor."

   The problem, the challenge, is the person in the mirror. And the solution is also the person in the mirror.

6. Remember, we are imprisoned by our weaknesses. We are liberated by our strengths.

7. Always remember, leadership is a lifestyle, not a characteristic.

I believe both of you are capable of understanding and practicing these truths, insights and principles and will see the multitude of benefits in passing them on.

Be prepared for rich and abundant living. It will surely happen.

Seth Taylor

CHAPTER XIV
HARVEY COLE TODAY

Several years have passed. Harvey has been promoted twice and is now executive vice president. When asked how he feels, he grins and says, "I'm full of it." And he certainly seems to be full of energy, full of health and full of joy. The years ahead look both prosperous and challenging. His family life grows richer, closer and stronger every day. Kevin, his oldest, just graduated from the International School of Business at the University of South Carolina. His other son was still in college and is a junior at the Citadel, and his daughter was head cheerleader at her high school in her senior year. One of Ellen's two daughters is a freshman at Lander University. Her other daughter is married and just had Harvey and Ellen's first grandchild.

He and Ellen along with Jean and Chuck and their families are closer than ever, and Harvey never overlooks an opportunity to tell others about what Jean did for him. Perhaps more important, he feels real pleasure every time he learns about another person being mentored by the mysterious Mr. Taylor and quietly chuckles to himself about the surprise they have in store.

He often wears the cuff links Mr. Taylor gave him, and every now and then, someone asks why he's wearing cuff links with the initials ST instead of HC. That usually leads him into telling them about the sheep thief and Mr. Taylor.

Recently, Harvey has begun to discover to his amazement and satisfaction that there are a growing number of people who are coming to HIM to get advice and counseling. He always responds positively and always feels honored that they want his help.

He's also usually the first to tell them that no one is born with all the answers and that he stays in growth mode. He also tells them that in order for Mr. Taylor, Jean or anyone else to have become a mentor, they must have usually survived a very difficult experience and, with the help and support of others, become a much stronger person than they would have without the experience.

Harvey continues to remind himself that the challenge was very clear. Since he was now a mentor himself, he must be willing to spend time with others and help them as Mr. Taylor helped him. Thus, the last great secret was realized.

Ultimate fulfillment came from passing all of this on to others.

ABOUT JOE BATTEN
1926–2006

JOE BATTEN was often introduced as America's premier authority on motivation. He spoke more than 3,000 times throughout the world in South and Central America and in countries that include South Africa, New Zealand, Ireland, and England. Joe was often introduced as one of the five leading management and leadership authorities in the world. He wrote the best-selling book *Tough-Minded Management*, translated into over 20 languages. He is the individual who gave the U.S. Army the phrase "Be All You Can Be." Joe wrote over three hundred articles for such publications as *Executive Excellence*, *Selling Power*, *The Christian Businessman*, *The ASTD Journal* and many more. He produced over forty-six videos, one of which, *Keep Reaching*, was voted "Motivational Film of the Year." His thirty audio programs include *How to Be a Master Motivator* and *The Greatest Secret*, while his nineteen books include *The Leadership Principles of Jesus*.

ABOUT AL WALKER

AL WALKER is president of his own training and development firm, Al Walker & Associates, Inc., an organization he founded in 1981 that specializes in skill-building training programs that help people be more productive in personal and organizational management, speaking skills, sales, sales management, leadership, customer service and personal development. Their program *Successful Selling Systems* has been used by some of America's premier businesses. They have conducted over two thousand training clinics, workshops, seminars and programs for organizations from the United States, Europe, Canada, Mexico and the Caribbean.

Al is also a motivational humorist who is a past president of The National Speakers Association and has served as chair of the NSA Foundation Board of Trustees. He has earned or been awarded every designation achievable in the speaking industry. He has twice received the NSA President's Award for distiguished service, is a Certified Speaking Professional, a member of the CPAE Speakers Hall of Fame, and is a recipient of The Master of Influence Award for his global impact through his speaking. He has also received the Cavett Award—the National Speakers Association's highest and most cherished award, presented annually to the member who has rendered exceptional service to the speaking industry and the association.